Rider by Night

Books by Karin Anckarsvard
available through Scholastic Book Clubs:
The Mysterious Schoolmaster
Rider by Night

Rider by Night

Karin Anckarsvärd

Illustrated by Charles W. Walker

Translated from the Swedish by
Annabelle MacMillan

SCHOLASTIC BOOK SERVICES

NEW YORK • TORONTO • LONDON • AUCKLAND • SYDNEY

© 1958 by Karin Anckarsvard. English translation.
© 1960 by Harcourt Brace Jovanovich, Inc. First published in Sweden under the title of Varfor just Krabat?

This edition is published by Scholastic Book Services, a division of Scholastic Magazines, Inc., by arrangement with Harcourt Brace Jovanovich, Inc.

1st printing................................January 1971

Printed in the U.S.A.

Contents

CHAPTER 1

Jenny Gerda Augusta

"The fact that it's happened—just plain happened, I mean—doesn't seem so strange. But the amazing thing, the really incredible thing, is that it's happened to me!"

Jenny curled up in one corner of the old-fashioned striped sofa in her bedroom and drew her knees up under her chin as she gazed out the window, straight into the blue horizon of the clear autumn afternoon.

She continued talking, mostly into space.

"Usually nothing ever happens to me—nothing either wonderful or unpleasant. It's always been Viveca that has things happen to her. And it's not that she ever does anything to deserve it, either. That's just the way it is. You can tell it just by her name. Viveca! They chose the name because it has such a pretty sound. Nobody in our family has ever been named that before. But Jenny! You can tell a mile away that I was named for an aunt. A name that's fine and honorable to carry with you through life. But definitely secondhand. And just to be on the safe side, they tacked on Gerda and Augusta too.

"Pooh!" Jenny suddenly swung her head around as if she had just been reminded that she was actually talking to a friend. "No, I'm not envious. It's just true. Everybody knows it. Viveca's blond and slender and tall and straight. Photographers drool just looking at her. In her free time she's a teen-age model—that's typical. And most of the time the phone almost rings itself off the wall with calls for her."

Jenny giggled. She knew that she was only sounding off. Her listener, Mariann, a contemporary of Jenny's who had golden, curly hair, a pointed chin, and small, bright eyes, remained silent. Perhaps she was trying to identify herself with the lucky Viveca.

"And when old Aunt Jenny died—she was grand-mother's sister—who do you think inherited the pearl necklace? Viveca! Who else? She was the oldest, and she looked like grandmother. What good was it then to be named after Aunt Jenny?"

Unexpectedly, Jenny bolted up from the sofa. She landed some distance out into the room, stretched her arms high over her head, and stood on her tiptoes as if, by simply being happy, she could hasten the process of grow-ing up.

"But it doesn't matter a bit any more. Pooh! A hundred clothes models and a hundred old pearl necklaces all locked up in jewel cases can't add up to having your own horse! And this isn't going to be just any old horse, either!"

"Sit down and tell me about it sensibly! I still don't have it all straight because you were talking in such fits and starts over the telephone. Are you going to own this horse, or are you going to borrow it, and what does it look like, and everything else?"

Jenny resumed her normal posture.

"Well, it's really going to be mine," she said, and as she finished this statement, which sounded a little bold, a little reckless, the tone of her voice sank as snow would sink into a valley. "I'll tell you everything from the beginning.

"You know that we have an uncle who owns a breeding farm down in the southern part of Sweden. He's had it for many years and has bred some fine horses there—mostly race horses. But it isn't so easy to make a living at that sort of thing here in this country, so when he got an offer to take some of his best stock with him and be the manager of a stable in Canada, he decided he would accept. The stable in Canada is very well known, and both he and his wife and Anders—my cousin—are very happy about it . . ."

Jenny stopped short and listened. From downstairs it sounded as if all the furniture in the house were being knocked over, and immediately following that there was the sound of someone running up the steps. She started to say something, but she decided against it, since there were screams and cries now to accompany the other sounds.

A moment later the door flew open and a small boy hurled himself into the room. Just outside the door the screams and cries had turned into something resembling syllables. Now they became real words.

"Snake . . . snake . . . that snake!"

"Lars!" said Jenny sharply. "Can't you see that I have company? What will Mariann think? Shame on you."

Lars caught his breath, pausing in the process to give Mariann a defiant look. As he pressed his lips together, he was obviously trying to decide whether to scream again or to give some real information. Mariann shook her blond head and somehow managed to halt the tidal wave.

"Don't mind about him, Jen. I know what small boys are like. What's the matter, Lars? Why are you so unhappy?"

"She is a snake," he announced, in full control of himself once again. "Viveca, I mean." His small, tender mouth began to tremble, and this, in combination with the remark he had made, caused Jenny's heart to melt.

"Tell us all about it, Lars," she said. "Sit down here beside Jenny and tell us. Why is Viveca a snake?" She lifted her little brother up onto the sofa beside her and pretended not to notice his muddy red boots.

"Okay, okay," said Lars. "I'm *going* to tell you. It was like this. We were talking about the horse—the one you're going to get from Uncle Karl. And I said that when it came, I was going to borrow it"—Lars glanced quickly at his sister to see how she was taking this announcement and continued hastily in order to anticipate any possible protests—"every day and ride and gallop all over Nordvik and even farther away than that. But then that snake said, 'Nobody will let you do that,' she said, 'because in the first place the horse will be frightened just looking at you, and he'll run away and hide . . . and . . . and . . . in the second place you're too fat and your legs are too short and you'll bounce off just like a bullet . . .'"

At this point Lars was overcome with sobs, but since he didn't want to lose the attention of his audience, he stifled the sobs and proceeded with his story. "But she was lying, wasn't she, Jenny? I can stay on great big horses all right, and you'll let me borrow it when it comes, Jen, won't you, huh, Jen, won't you?"

Above his round, ash-blond head, Jenny and Mariann exchanged glances.

Jenny thought to herself, "He's just like I was a few minutes ago. He doesn't come right out and say it, but he's thinking pretty much as I did—that it's always someone else who gets everything, that it's always Viveca who has all the luck, and that he never, never does." It was not very pleasant to feel that way; it made everything more complicated than was necessary. Viveca never had to be bothered with that kind of thinking . . .

Jenny noticed suddenly that Mariann was avoiding her glance. Could it be that she too . . . ? But they were such good friends! Mariann couldn't be jealous.

Jenny banished the disturbing thought from her mind.

"You have to *learn* to ride, Lars. I have been riding for many, many years . . ."

"Two!" Lars promptly corrected her.

"Well, yes, but I've taken many, many lessons. You have to *learn* to ride, you see, just as you have to learn to read and to write and to drive an automobile."

"Someday Lars will have the chance to learn, too," Mariann said. She had gotten up and had begun to examine Jenny's bookcase.

A certain feeling of uneasiness filled the room. Was it really possible that Mariann, as well as Lars, felt a little sting of envy? Perhaps it wasn't such a good idea to talk

too much with someone else about the thing that made
you so indescribably happy.

As she rested her chin on the top of Lars's head, Jenny
said, "You'll get your chance to learn. And then you can
borrow my horse and ride—very carefully, of course—because you have to be very cautious with a fine horse."

She stopped short. Perhaps she shouldn't have used the
word "fine."

Mariann looked up.

"Do you think it will be a race horse? A thoroughbred?"

Jenny was now on guard.

"I just don't know. I'm going down and choose it myself.
The most important thing, Uncle Karl says, is that I take
one that is suitable for me. I'm getting this horse, you see,
because he and I are the only ones in the whole family—
except Lars of course—who care anything about horses,
and because he wants to leave one horse here so that he
can ride if he comes back on a visit sometime."

"But obviously the loveliest and most expensive horse
will be the one that will suit you best," said Mariann with
a little laugh.

Jenny shut her eyes and buried her nose in Lars's hair.
Amazingly enough, it smelled pretty good.

"I don't know . . ."

She was glad when Lars interrupted.

"We are going to have a big, *nice* horse!" he said hap-
pily. "When can I come to the stable and begin to learn,
Jenny? I'll have to hurry if I'm going to be ready in time.
Jenny, tell me!"

"But, Lars, you are only seven years old. I was ten when I rode a big horse for the first time, and I was just plain lucky that everything went all right, I'll tell you. Now you run along. Mariann and I want some time to ourselves."

Lars dug the heels of his boots into the edge of the sofa.

"Not before you promise."

"Promise what?"

"That I can come along with you to the stable next time."

The two pairs of eyes met. Jenny's were clear and dark blue; Lars's were steel gray and clouding up with every second that passed. Had they been alone, a long discussion would have ensued—agitated on one side, and calm, but firm, on the other. But as it was now, the battle was confined to the eyes.

The result was just as they both knew it would be.

"Okay, you can come along."

All at once the heels of the boots were no longer digging into the sofa. They were flying, on wings of triumph, toward the door.

"Jenny, you're wonderful. Thank you, Jenny. Thank you so much, Jenny . . ."

With a meaningful smile Mariann shut the door.

"Now you've let yourself in for it. What do you think the riding instructor is going to say when you come to the stable dragging along a little fellow like that?"

Jenny shrugged her shoulders. They were broad and straight, contrasting strongly with her round throat and her small, dark head. She came to a decision, in silent opposition to Mariann's superior manner, that Lars would have a royal time on a real horse.

"Oh, it will work out all right," she answered matter-of-factly. "We can try to get Manilla or some other horse that's as peaceful as a camel for him, and if worst comes to worst, I can lead the horse."

"Great fun!" Mariann commented sourly. She picked up her bookbag, which she had carelessly thrown down by the door. "Well, Jen, I have to go home and study my math, that's for sure. I'll probably be hearing more about your wonderful thoroughbred after you have selected it, I guess."

". . . your wonderful thoroughbred . . ."

The words echoed and returned to haunt Jenny as, somewhat later, she sat at her rickety, hand-me-down desk. She hadn't once said that it was going to be a thoroughbred, let alone referred to it as wonderful. Mariann was a little jealous, that was obvious. Not terribly, but enough so that she was pleased at the trouble Jenny had had with her little brother. Mariann herself had just one brother—older and nearly grown up. Quite a feather in the cap of a teenage girl in a small town!

Jenny looked down at her composition book. It was in sad shape, full of finished exercises done in heavy black pencil, complete with dog-eared pages and a torn label. All of Jenny's books were dog-eared. She wrote, it seemed, only with dull pencils, and her written words had the qualities of whirling dervishes.

Looking up, she found, to her surprise, that with her right hand she had unconsciously been drawing the head of a horse on her new notebook. It wasn't a very good drawing. The horse looked comical and deformed, and Jenny laughed out loud.

At that point she remembered her teacher in Swedish grammar, and immediately went to work with her eraser. She did a pretty good job of erasing the horse's head, but she noticed that the notebook no longer looked new.

CHAPTER 2

Excerpts

From Viveca Tornquist's Diary

Oct. 3 Fed up with everything. Chemistry in the morning, and the little kids are always making so much noise in the hall that I can't concentrate. Was down and tried on the new "sack" dress which they just got in at Ekebergs. Fitted beautifully, and it was just the right color—not shocking pink, and not strawberry, but something in between. It will look fine on me even if I am blond. Price is decent. I have 30 crowns left from my baby-sitting money, and mother will give me 30.

But the neckline was all wrong. The same old, eternal shirt collar. The saleslady said, "Gives it just the right sporty touch." Naturally she wanted to sell it. The collar was too big, and it had an idiotic binding around the edge which ruined everything. Got a "B" in English.

Oct. 7 Certain that my hair has gotten darker since last summer. Will try the lemon rinse. I don't believe all these tales about the strong beer stuff. For that matter, I could only try it if there were an open bottle. If I opened one, Papa would raise the roof. Even now he thinks that Mrs. Johansson has begun to take a few nips, but they want to keep her here to help with the housework, so everybody's keeping quite quiet about that.

Oct. 9 Olof called. He is going to have a party on Saturday, but he has invited Fatty Patty, so that's the end of that. Their mothers know each other. I've always said that Olof is no kind of boy friend to have around!

Barbara said that Mariann's big brother Bill said that Jenny is chic. CHIC! Well, I suppose so if you think it's chic to have hair that smells of horses from five miles away, or to move like an elephant. Then Jenny is 100 per cent chic. But that child *can* pull herself together when she makes up her mind. Of course, she's been totally unconscious now for two weeks—ever since the letter came from Uncle Karl. Everybody at school says the same. "Pelleponasus," the teacher we both have in biology, asked me if my little sister had ever had her ears examined. He said he was of the opinion that such an examination should really take place—that's the way he expresses himself—because when he had asked Jen's class what animal was closest to man with respect to intelligence and had gone on to say that they stand upright and that they could learn to manage both a knife and a fork, Jenny had raised her hand and answered, "The horse." The living end, she is!

Going to wear my light blue this Saturday. Kristofer is coming. He has his good points. I got A-minus in Swedish. "Mature treatment of the subject," the teacher said.

I'll buy some bubble bath at the drugstore and use it with my bath on Friday evening. Everything is so dead!

*   *   *

From Jenny Tornquist's Diary
My First Diary
HORSES!!!!!
HORSE DIARY
Hippology

Sept. 9 The first time I rode was when I was about five years old. I rode a horse named Lola, out in the country at Uncle Karl's place. The second time I rode I was ten years old. Then I rode a Gotland pony. Since that time I have been at Nordvik's Stables almost all the time when I haven't been in school, and I've helped to lead the beginners, clean the hoofs, saddle and unsaddle the horses, and give them sugar. On my eleventh birthday, one of my presents was riding lessons. I have now ridden over a year and more than sixty times. The fourth time I rode I galloped.

I assembled my equipment gradually. First I got a whip, riding pants six months later, and then spurs. Now I am saving up to buy a jockey cap with a helmet in it.

Sept. 12 My favorite horses at the riding academy are Hoppsan (out of Topper-Dinah), 108, Tarantella, and Java. Hoppsan is eight years old. She is so sweet I just can hardly believe it.

Sept. 14 I have now fallen off for the first time. I was riding Paulette, the fastest of all the horses at the stables. I had never galloped back to the stable with her before. After two times around the ring, Java, who was right in front of us, began to slow down in order to heed a call of nature. So did Paulette. Java took off at a gallop again, but Paulette didn't follow suit. Then I gave her a kick—which she isn't used to—and whether it was because of that or because the other horses were so far ahead, I don't know, but suddenly she took off at a wild clip. For half a lap everything turned black in front of my eyes. Then I flew over her head. I landed with a thud in some tan-bark. Heard Paulette's hoofs rumbling, and I thought to myself, "My last moment on earth has really arrived."

But it hadn't; Paulette halted right in front of me. I was sore in the strangest places for three days afterward. I really felt as if I had tried to fly.

Sept. 16 I haven't had time to write that we have begun to jump. We began with cavalletis and brush jumps. I had Tarantella the first time.

We have also ridden in drill. We have learned "column left single file at the trot," "left turn," "column right and left," "by twos," "twos right," and "on front into line." And we have learned to listen for the word "ho" at the end of the command.

Sept. 19 Last Friday at the Youth Center I saw a movie about horses. It dealt with the origin of the horse. It pointed out that the first horses looked like foxes and that they were only a little over a yard long. I've seen a sculpture of a horse which was done by a Japanese artist. It was tall, and its legs were low, and it looked more like the forerunners of the horse than like our horses.

Today we had composition again. I knew before I handed it in that mine wasn't any good. There were only three subjects to choose from: "Different Ways to Have Fun with a Ball," "The Fall Teen-Age Fashions" (if only it could have been "Fall Teen-Age Riding Fashions"!), and "Martin Luther." I was forced to write about old Luther, and it was awful. The teacher said that "it displayed abysmal ignorance and lack of maturity."

Hoppsan was lame for a while, but now she is fine again. She is a bay with a star on her forehead. She is my very favorite horse!

September 23. September 23. SEPTEMBER 23!

A letter came today. Because of this, September 23 appears three times, once with capital letters, on this page. The letter is from Uncle Karl. He is the most wonderful,

nicest, best person who ever lived, and I don't believe I
will ever be unhappy again in my life.

Don't have time to write any more today because we
are expecting a phone call from Uncle Karl. Will explain
everything later.

CHAPTER 3

Big and Little Events at the Stables

"How old did you say the little guy is? Seven?"

The riding instructor scratched the back of his neck and amusedly looked Lars up and down, from his thick-soled shoes, which had only a few inches of his socks peeping above them, all the way up to his hand-knitted stocking cap.

The uninhibited Lars, on the other hand, took a good look at the riding instructor, but Lars's perspective, of course, was decidedly oblique and somewhat distorted, since the riding instructor was a good deal over and above medium height. He was a slight man who looked to be in his early forties. However, if you stopped to think of how many years he had been giving instructions in riding, you would undoubtedly realize that he was much older. The combination of daily contact with young people and with horses must have been the secret of his youthful appearance.

Jenny felt rather embarrassed. She didn't mind so much that she would probably have to take care of both Lars and the horse he would be riding instead of riding herself, but she realized how small and young Lars must look to

the riding instructor. However, as she knew very well, the only thing that would convince Lars about the difficulties of riding a big horse would be for him to come face to face with the cold, hard facts.

The riding instructor, who understood many things besides horses, suddenly became serious.

"Jenny, it's a shame," he said, "that I don't have room to keep some ponies here. Many boys and girls of this age come and beg to begin taking lessons. But when you're as little as this boy is, you can't begin with a full-grown horse. He hasn't enough strength to make the horse respect him. And if he were to try to ride a big horse, the result would be easy to guess: he would get frightened, and that fear could linger on."

Lars's big eyes betrayed his disappointment, but not to the extent that Jenny had feared. She had figured it out correctly. It was much easier to listen to a big, strong man in riding breeches, a man who took Lars's hopes seriously, than to his sister who could be mistakenly accused of selfish motives.

"Come again in a couple of years," the riding instructor said. "And grow up real big during that time. Well, O.K., Jenny, if you'll take the responsibility for him and lead his horse, he can go around with the beginners' group today. Take Manilla. She's gentle. That way, fellow, you won't have come all the way over here for nothing."

They walked together toward the stalls, Lars with careful steps. Jenny's face showed a great sense of relief, while on Lars's face there was nothing but pure devotion.

"Hi," someone said.

They met Mariann leading Beauty, the stable's most magnificent thoroughbred. She was going to be the head rider for the beginners' group.

Coquettishly, Beauty lowered her head. Her mane shone, and her long, black tail swept proudly by Jenny, who giggled softly. She knew that Mariann skipped swimming class, the last period at school, and devoted herself entirely to Beauty's care and grooming. Nobody at the stables had such a natural way with the horses as did Mariann. She had calmness, stamina, and patience.

In a few minutes Lars was proudly leading the even-tempered Manilla, who probably could have found the way to the ring by herself, even walking in her sleep. Lars petted Manilla's soft nose, and watchful and alert, took his place in the procession at the door. Two Scotties and a cat moved around freely among the horses' hoofs and the legs of the riders. But even they felt an obvious responsibility for their behavior.

Ten horses now formed a line in the middle of the ring. A tall boy, who had previously been in trouble with both the children's court and the police, lifted Lars gently and carefully up into the saddle. Toward the far wall Mariann's blond hair and Beauty's dark mane glistened. Just as quietly as a well-oiled machine the lesson had begun.

Ten horses, head to tail, marched out toward the far side of the ring. Ten riders, both boys and girls, displayed postures ranging all the way from a sack of potatoes to the proper position, the latter represented by Mariann alone.

Last in line came Jenny, leading Manilla. She hoped

to persuade the horse to trot along evenly and maintain that speed.

Lars looked puzzled. He was suddenly aware that Manilla was very tall and very broad, and that the sawdust-covered ground was a long distance away. His dreams of horses and of riding had been too strongly influenced by the zoo's small, shaggy ponies, and by beautiful little toy horses. Reality was fascinating but overwhelming. He heard the riding instructor's directions, but he was too overcome to be able to follow them.

However, Manilla soon saw through the situation. By disposition she was phlegmatic, to be sure, but not so much so that she wasn't going to make the most of an opportunity when it came her way. As long as Jenny ran ahead and led her, she trotted nicely, but the moment Jenny let go of the reins, thinking that rider and horse ought to be able to get along by themselves, Manilla slowed down. Cautiously and doubtfully Lars kicked her sides with his heels, but Manilla remained indifferent, took another couple of steps just to be on the safe side, and then halted altogether. Jenny rushed over. But the whole equestrian parade got out of order. Only Mariann and Beauty continued with impassive elegance.

The riding instructor's voice rang out. "Keep on riding! Ride. Ride! Hurry up, Birgit! Shorten your reins, Eva! Sit up straight. That's fine, Peter. Now we'll try trotting."

Jenny ran and ran. She was flushed, and drops of perspiration formed along her forehead.

When Gunilla, one of the girls hired by the stables, yelled out that there was a phone call for the riding instructor, Jenny decided to take a well-earned rest. She led Manilla into the middle of the ring, where she stopped.

"You're sure stupid today, Manilla," she said, gasping for breath. But, in any case, she took a piece of sugar out of her pocket. "Well, Lars, how does it feel?"

Lars never even got a chance to answer because at that moment something happened. A break in the procession had occurred when Manilla and Lars had left it. The horse behind them had been Palma, who evidently felt that her comrades had disappeared into the distance and deserted her. Simultaneously she missed the disciplining presence of the riding instructor and decided, come what might, to catch up with the rest. She took off at such a clip that she managed to bump Paulette, who, in turn, began to speed up.

Jenny remarked afterwards that for a brief while she had the feeling that it was raining beginners. Actually, only three landed in the tanbark, and this with a minimum of fuss.

But one of the horses, a newcomer to the stables, backed up suddenly, hitting Beauty, who bucked.

Mariann was taken by surprise.

Over the horse's head she flew in an arch and landed on her side near the wall.

It had been a long time since the well-run stable in Nordvik had witnessed anything like this—riderless horses, wide-eyed beginners, and horses neighing wildly.

Hoppsan, who was hungry, saw her chance and simply

walked straight out of the ring, back through the door to her stall, where she began to eat some hay. The beginner in the saddle, an eleven-year-old girl cried, laughed, begged, and pleaded. But Hoppsan continued to eat.

During all this time Gunilla and Jenny worked desperately in an attempt to create order out of the chaos. Luckily, Manilla stood so calmly in place that Jenny dared to let go of her reins. She managed to catch Beauty and to calm her down by talking to her reassuringly. Two of the riders who had been thrown off rose out of the tanbark, covered with dirt, and mounted again, while the third went out to tend to a scratch on his wrist.

It was only after the arena had once again gotten back to normal that Jenny remembered Mariann.

She had managed to get up, but she was leaning against the wall. Quickly Jenny ran over to her.

"How did it happen? It looked pretty awful."

"There's nothing wrong with me," Mariann said, but Jenny noticed that Mariann remained motionless. "I had no idea what was happening before she bucked, and then I didn't have a chance. I didn't hit myself anywhere, but I must have landed with my foot under me. It feels just peculiar enough that I don't think I'd better stand on it too much."

At this point the riding instructor came over to join them. Upon his return, everyone, horses and children alike, had tried to get back into place and to appear as if everything were just as it should be and as if nothing whatever had happened, but riderless horses were not easy to hide. Gunilla, who finally managed to get the contrary

Hoppsan out of her stall, gave a short summary of the events.

"I am absolutely O.K.," Mariann said firmly. "I'll just rest my foot for a while. Jenny can help me go out."

The riding instructor looked sharply at Mariann. He could understand that she didn't want sympathy, and he had respect for courage.

"O.K.," he said hurriedly. "Gunilla, lead Beauty out."

Bengt, the boy with the troubled past, offered to take care of Manilla and Lars.

As soon as they disappeared from the ring, Mariann limping and Jenny supporting her, the well-ordered, smooth parade, accompanied by the muffled sound of hoofs, got in motion again around the outer edge of the arena.

"What a circus!" Jenny commented, as she helped Mariann into a chair inside the office. "It was that crazy Palma's fault, all of it. How does your foot feel?"

"Aw, there's nothing really wrong. I'm going to take a look at it."

Mariann pulled off her boot. As she cautiously moved her foot, she winced with pain. Jenny saw that the foot was swollen.

"I think you'd better go see the doctor about this," she said. "It probably isn't broken, but you should have some sort of bandage."

Jenny looked sideways at Mariann. Her soft skin was pale and white.

"Say, Mariann, are you scared? I'll gladly ride in with you if you want me to."

Mariann suddenly shook her head wildly.

"How stupid do you think I am? A foot like this is certainly nothing to be afraid of."

Her voice betrayed her concern, and the look on her face, to Jenny's surprise, was almost bitter.

Jenny asked, "Shall I call for a taxi?"

"Yes, please do."

She curtly refused Jenny's help and her company and limped out through the gate all by herself.

A couple of times, through the branches of the lindens, Jenny could see the rear lights on the taxi as it swung with the curves on the road leading away from the stables. At the entrance to the ring she remained a moment, deep in thought. What had gotten into Mariann? Her foot hurt her, of course. But still . . . Mariann was usually a past master at the difficult art of self-control. Too bad. She probably wouldn't be able to ride for a while.

A tremor, a feeling that she had been very lucky, passed through Jenny's whole body. Just three more days and then she would go down to the southern part of Sweden and select her horse. Her own horse. Far away she could hear Lars's clear, childish voice:

"Look, Bengt. She's moving. We're moving all by ourselves."

CHAPTER 4

The Choice

On the way through Vesterlen Jenny saw the sea. It came into view unexpectedly, calm and elephant-gray, beyond a huge orchard, and the picture of it was, for some reason, the only one that remained with her after the whole of her quick trip to southern Sweden. There were the small, leafless, dark trees, all in straight rows, the black, plowed furrows, and suddenly the sea broadly and softly embracing the land.

The feeling of excitement, which she hadn't been able to stifle ever since the school bell had rung after her last class yesterday, and which remained during the few short hours of sleep she had had the night before, had finally disappeared.

"Look. Can you see the sea from here? I had forgotten about that."

Uncle Karl, who was driving, turned toward her for a second and noticed the dimples in her cheeks.

"You catch glimpses of it now and then," he replied. "Tell me, Jenny, what do they think about this horse back home? Are Lars and Viveca jealous?"

"I really don't know. Viveca isn't, anyway. She has so many other things to think about, and besides she isn't like that. Lars almost thinks that it's he who is going to get the horse. Everybody is already pretty used to the idea, I guess. But I still think it's a miracle, I really do."

Uncle Karl's complexion, tanned and somewhat wrinkled, was that of a man who had spent much time out of doors. He laughed now and, as he did so, still more lines appeared around his eyes and at the corners of his mouth. But what he said, strangely enough, was serious.

"You regard it as a miracle. But I'm going to tell you a secret. The miracle is not just the fact that you wake up one morning suddenly owning a horse There is something more to the story—or, rather, there was."

Jenny looked questioningly at her uncle. He noticed her bewilderment and continued talking while they slowly drove under the arches and through the shadows of the surrounding forest of beech trees.

"A miracle occurs here on earth, I believe, when a person does something fine and right and completely unselfish for another person. Your father did something like that once for me. I've never been able to forget it. It doesn't really matter what it was all about. For me, at least, it was a miracle, and I want you to know that this is the reason you woke up the other morning owning a horse. . . . Now you can see Vernestad right over there."

Jenny touched Uncle Karl's elbow lightly. It was very seldom that he talked so long at one time, and certainly never about anything that couldn't be seen or touched— only about saddles, new foals, and similar nice things.

Jenny felt as if she understood Uncle Karl, and she liked the idea.

Later, as they were going through the stalls, he didn't have much to say. What he said came out in brief sentences and had to do with everyday things.

"It's a good thing you remembered to bring your helmet with you! . . . Here is where we built the addition last spring. . . . This filly is out of my English import Pillar. . . . Most of the horses are already out—down there in the meadow. We'll go down there a little later on."

They stopped by the stalls where the rasp of leather straps could be heard and where Jenny could see the large brown eyes of the horses.

"When it comes right down to it, there probably aren't too many horses for you to choose among. Yours should be the right height and the right age. Naturally you'll have to both ride and practice jumping with them to see how it goes. I'll also ride them so that you can see how they look in motion."

They walked across the wet, tufted grass, down toward the fenced-in field where the horses were. From a pond where the sparrows were taking their morning baths a mist rose. The horses were far away on the other side of the meadow, but as soon as one of them caught sight of the people approaching and set off at a gallop, the others trooped after him.

"You'll have to take a look at both of these half-thoroughbreds. They're nice. Both are out of my own Patrick, and Ruter was the mare. She is a magnificent horse but perhaps a bit too nervous."

"I saw her inside the stall," Jenny said. "She was just beautiful."

Uncle Karl gave her a look that was full of understanding. All this time Jenny, whose pockets bulged with sugar lumps, was as busy as she could be. She noticed the half-thoroughbreds that Uncle Karl had mentioned. Both of them were bays. One had a curious, curly mane, which stood straight up, and a white streak on her nose, a combination that made her look very mischievous.

At first all the horses crowded around Uncle Karl, but when they noticed Jenny's load of sugar, they switched their allegiance to her. She petted a throat here, stroked a head there, and moved freely among them in order to be able to compare the horses better. The two half-thoroughbreds were standing a little in front of the others, but as Jenny took a step backward, another horse crowded in, putting her head between them. This one was also a bay, but lighter in color with warm, gleaming copper tones.

Jenny observed that there was an unusual width between this horse's eyes, which gave her a look of wisdom and gentleness.

As the other horses stepped aside, the newcomer nuzzled Jenny, obviously in search of sugar. It was quite evident that this horse was aware of the place where sugar could generally be found because she immediately nuzzled against the pocket of Jenny's jacket.

Jenny began to laugh.

"Look here. Take it easy, you rascal. Help yourself to the sugar, but you don't have to eat my hand too."

Uncle Karl took the horse by the halter.

"That was real intuition, as they say, Jenny. Her name actually is Rascal."

"Isn't that funny? But Rascal seems to me more like a boy's name."

"I agree with you about that. But Anders said almost the same thing as you did—'Such a lively rascal!'—right after she was born, and later we named her Rascal. She's a lovely filly."

Jenny thought to herself, "Now, don't be stupid. You judge much too much by appearances, both with animals and with people. And you haven't even really seen this horse yet."

"Is Rascal also a half-thoroughbred?" she asked aloud.

"Yes. Out of Pillar and Vernestad's Dame. She has the lantern-shaped marking on her forehead, and she's pretty attractive, don't you think so?"

Jenny hadn't concerned herself much with the markings.

"Her eyes are so well placed," she said, secretly hoping that Rascal was among those few of Uncle Karl's horses that might be suitable for her. Rascal turned her head toward Jenny and pricked up her ears. She wasn't about to let herself be crowded out by the other horses.

Later, with the assistance of Uncle Karl and Anders, the trial rides took place. But by then Jenny had already seen Rascal trotting around the meadow, lightly, energetically, and stepping high, but all of the while balanced and able to take care of herself. She begged to saddle Rascal herself.

She rode and jumped with both the other half-thorough-breds and also with a couple of thoroughbreds, but with Rascal she rode far out into the fields and on into the woods where the beech trees were.

Uncle Karl, riding Patrick, came to meet her, and they rode slowly home side by side. Uncle Karl remarked, "I was puzzled when you expressed the desire to saddle her, and I thought, 'Why Rascal in particular?' I had thought that she was a little too big for you, but your legs are long, and they'll grow to be even longer. Rascal will be six years old in June. Perhaps she is a bit young, but she has an un-usually fine character and disposition. I trained her my-self. And now I see that she's just right for you."

Jenny petted Rascal's copper-colored neck. After every-one was out of earshot, she whispered, "Rascal, you won-derful Golden Bay. Rascal, you're the right one for me. Jenny's Rascal."

It was decided that Rascal would be sent up a couple of weeks later with an animal transport as soon as a stall be-came free in the Nordvik stables.

CHAPTER 5

The Morning Ride

The whole household was asleep when Jenny tiptoed down the stairs in her stocking feet. Through a half-open door she saw Mona, her five-year-old sister, pink and white, sleeping peacefully in her equally pink-and-white bed. Mona resembled a rosebud when she fell asleep in the evening, and, as she lay there in the morning, she was just as sweet and motionless, still covered by her blankets and sheets.

Lars, on the other hand, fought at the mere idea of going to bed, fought falling asleep, and slept with a fight. His bed always had a perfectly shameful appearance. That morning only he and the mattress were left in the bed. The pillows had landed far out on the floor. The sheets had disappeared.

Jenny's sleepy thoughts dwelt a while on this mystery but came to no conclusion.

There was an aura of peace and happy unconsciousness following her as she rode her bicycle through the city's deserted streets. A couple of blackbirds hopped busily underneath a hedge, but she saw scarcely a living thing until she came to the old, overgrown garden beyond the lumberyard. There, she and the occupant of the garden, a huge

German hare, paid their morning respects to each other
—that is to say, the hare pricked up his ears, and Jenny
leaned over her handle bars pretending not to see him.
On the first mornings they had met, he had scurried away,
but now he stayed on, convinced that Jenny was both blind
and deaf.

The clock on the weather-beaten facade of the Nordvik
castle said a quarter after six.

But at the stables the day had already begun. Gunilla
was currying Palma. Bengt was cleaning the stalls.

Rascal had quickly learned to be on the lookout for
Jenny. One brisk day, she had neighed when she caught
sight of Jenny.

Bengt had looked up covertly from his broom and had
muttered something about "lucky girl who doesn't even
begin to understand . . ." What it was Jenny didn't understand managed to escape her.

Now Bengt did not look up. He stuck closely to his work
and pretended not to hear Jenny's "Good morning," and
"Hi, there." Just at that point Rascal poked her nose
against Jenny's gray jacket.

"You can have the privilege of cleaning Rascal's stall
today yourself," Bengt muttered sourly. "I don't have time
to . . ."

The remainder of his words died away into a murmur.
Jenny held her peace. She knew that Bengt was usually in
a terrible mood in the mornings.

Gunilla methodically continued the process of grooming. She was a strong and well-developed girl. Though she

was slow in motion, she was invariably calm and just as invariably conscientious about her work.

The job of cleaning the stall, which usually fell upon Bengt as the extra employee at the stables, took Jenny a little longer than she had counted on. She noticed that it had previously not been very carefully cleaned in the corners. But she said nothing and didn't appear to be concerned. Luckily, her class would have a cooking lesson that day, which meant that school would begin a half hour later than usual. A whole hour for riding lay before her.

The wonderful moments of saddling Rascal were over. The leather straps creaked, and her hoofs tapped in a calm rhythm against the old wooden floor. In the gray dawn Jenny and Rascal stood atop the stable hill. It had not rained during the night, but the mist was heavy. Dew dropped from the drainpipes and from the bare, autumnal branches. The stable cat came sneaking around the corner, his stomach distended from his nightly hunt for mice. He was on the way to his favorite place in the hayloft but decided to go over first and say hello to Gunilla and to feel a little human warmth. Even a cat finds this helpful sometimes if he is to sleep well.

Jenny sat up straight. Rascal lowered her head and shook it.

On this hazy morning it seemed as if the copper sheen on her mane were actually giving off heat. She radiated eagerness and contentment with her environment.

At a walking pace they went down the hill, over the railroad tracks, toward the city. Both girl and horse were long-

ing to take off at a gallop. For that reason they took a short
cut through the community out to Nordvik's broad high-
way, which led from the main road down to the seashore.
Double rows of birches bordered the road. Riding was allowed between the white lines. There was the rich, musty
smell of soil from an adjacent, newly plowed field. The
soil was still loose, and it hadn't as yet hardened in the
frosty weather.

The breeze as they galloped caused Jenny to feel how
much mist and dampness were still in the air. The mois-
ture brushed softly against her cheeks and forehead.

The road extended over half a mile, straight and well-
built, and it led to the sea. But Jenny and Rascal couldn't
have cared less about the seashore. The beach was pebbly
and the nearby road was paved. They turned toward land
again, for now they wanted to go into the woods, to the
paths that were cushioned with moss and pine needles.
They walked an easy pace; both of them were warm and
out of breath.

A few moments later they met the first pedestrian of the
morning—a tall boy in a tweed jacket. Back of him, in the
ditch, his big Boxer was scratching and rooting around.
Jenny knew who he was, just as you usually know the
names of your schoolmates who somehow don't fit into
the ordinary pattern, even if they aren't in your class. He
was Kristofer Seaberg, a student a couple of grades ahead
of Jenny, president of the school's nature study group.

Kristofer and Jenny nodded to each other. The dog, who
went by the strange name of Ramrod, gave Rascal just one
uneasy glance and quickly looked the other way. Ramrod

was always apprehensive about any animal who was bigger than he.

Rascal began trotting along a path bordered by small pines.

A couple of seconds later Jenny caught herself musing on the fact that there was a certain something about old greenish-gray tweed jackets—weren't they about the same color as moss?—and that there was a certain something, too, about boys whose hair was just a little unkempt.

As Kristofer continued, he had a startlingly clear picture before him, this picture that a few minutes earlier had emerged from the trees—the head of a horse, with blue-and-white striped harness, the horse's look of contentment as she blinked her huge, brown eyes, her well-groomed, harmoniously built body, her neat hoofs, the long, sweeping tail. Just as clearly, he could see the girl's wide and motionless shoulders, her smooth, shiny, chestnut-brown hair.

He made up his mind that when he got home, he would begin reading the book on horse shows that he had just gotten.

Ramrod came bounding over with an old knotted branch in his mouth. He was overjoyed that the horse had disappeared, for now he was again the biggest animal in the woods. He showed the branch to Kristofer as if to say that if Kris were really nice, perhaps—but only perhaps—he would receive that fine, elegant, unique branch as a present from Ramrod.

In silence Rascal carried Jenny farther along the paths, bright with pine needles, and over the mossy flats. This was the best part of the morning ride. The air felt warm, they still had a half hour's freedom with one another, and the smell of the woods was precisely as it should be.

Eventually they came to the residential areas again. Here Nordvik's terrain stretched out a tentacle on which were small lots with tiny gray and red brick houses. Outside one of them Jenny slowed down. It would soon be seven-thirty, and signs of life were evident in several places.

Cautiously Jenny rode up to a small gravel path in the middle of a newly seeded lawn. Up in the gable of the house was an open window. Jenny halted Rascal.

"Mariann," she said softly. Then a little louder. "Mariann. . . ."

Outside the window a thin white curtain flapped like a sail. A blue jacket and a blond head appeared at the window.

"Hey, are you awake?"

Mariann replied with a huge yawn.

"Hi."

Everything was quiet. For some reason Jenny had to search for a subject of conversation. Just to break the silence she said something that immediately thereafter she wished that she had left unsaid.

"Why don't you come to the stables any more? I never see you."

Mariann rested the palms of her hands on the window sill. There, right before her eyes, was the same picture that Kristofer had carried away with him, and, at the same time, the smell of the horse hit her. It came crowding far into her room.

"It's no use. They won't let me ride, ever again, and I guess it probably doesn't matter."

Jenny's eyes opened wide.

"They won't let you? But why, for heaven's sake? You're getting along so well in school." This was Jenny's only concern, because Rascal, her beloved Rascal, did take time away from her studies. Several times lately Jenny had fallen asleep over her homework.

"Oh, it's not that," said Mariann curtly. "Mother has always been scared to death of everything to do with horses, and when this business happened with my foot, she nearly went out of her mind. She keeps saying that it could just as easily have been my neck. That's all there is to it."

"But your foot's O.K. now, isn't it?"

"Oh, sure. It's O.K. It was just sprained."

Again there was silence. For the life of her, Jenny couldn't think of a thing to say. Naturally, once more she said something that she almost immediately regretted

"That's a real shame, Mariann. For you. You're so wonderful at riding! I had just thought . . ."

Jenny stopped herself just in time. She was just about to say something about Mariann borrowing Rascal and exercising her when Jenny had a specially hard homework assignment or something of the sort.

Mariann's expression was peculiar. She gazed into space, straight out over Rascal's head, as if she didn't see a thing.

"Aw," she said, "it's too stupid and stinking and dopey for words—the whole thing. I get so mad I could spit . . ."

Jenny, who almost dropped her gloves in amazement at Mariann's outburst, didn't hear the end of the sentence because Mariann closed the window. The thin curtain got caught, and part of it was still flapping outside.

Jenny had never before heard such language coming from this well-brought-up girl. The bitterness in her voice seemed to go straight through Jenny's heavy jacket, even though the mist hadn't been able to penetrate it all morning. Rascal scraped her feet in the gravel. Could her horse also sense the unrest and desperation that poured out through the window even more obviously than the white curtain in the morning breeze?

Slowly horse and rider turned around. Slowly they rode along the bare roads, wet in the autumn morning, back to the stable.

CHAPTER 6

The Secret Club Strikes

"Jenny. Wake up. Jenny, girl—hey, wake up!"

The light from the lamp on the night table shone on Jenny's face. She opened her eyes. Pulled so forcefully out of the deepest valley of sleep, she could neither understand nor see anything.

"Sweetie, it's awful to have to waken you this way, but I've got to have someone to help me. Daddy's away, as you know, and tomorrow morning—I mean this morning— Viveca has an examination in Swedish, and she had such a hard time getting to sleep yesterday evening."

Jenny's head lay quietly on the pillow. Slowly, however, her blue eyes began to sparkle in their normal fashion, and now she opened them a little more widely. She noticed that the winter darkness still pushed heavily against the latticed windows and that her mother's face was ashen against her dark hair and her red robe.

"What is it?"

"It's Lars. I'm worried to death. I can't find him."

"Didn't he go to bed?"

"Of course. He went to bed last night as usual. He was sleeping like a log when I looked in on him at nine-thirty. But now the bed is empty."

Jenny was overcome with bewilderment and sleepiness. However, she had to make an effort to understand the puzzle.

"What time is it?"

"Four. A quarter after. I've been searching for him for a long time."

Jenny now slipped on her yellow bathrobe and stuck her trembling feet into her slippers. Through the window she could see the light down by the road, and against the light she could see the snowflakes cascading down. Hurrying, she followed her mother who was half running through the corridor down toward the children's room.

"Has it been snowing long?"

"It must have been. The ground is completely covered."

They stood beside Lars's bed, which, as usual, looked as if it had just been struck by an earthquake. Mechanically Jenny poked her feet among the covers, which had been thrown off onto the floor. You never knew where he might land.

"Do you suppose he's been sleepwalking? Have you ever seen him walk in his sleep?"

Jenny shook her head. Following a hunch, she suddenly bent down and peeked under the bed. All that was there were two tops and a toy automobile without wheels.

Mrs. Tornquist clasped her hands to her chest. Simultaneously their eyes met, and they looked over to the other part of the room where Mona was sleeping, peacefully, quietly, as usual.

"Maybe she saw or heard something?" Jenny suggested. "Can't we wake her up and ask her?"

Mrs. Tornquist sat down on the edge of the bed and brushed a lock of hair away from Mona's forehead. Cautiously she moved Mona's soft little arms, which were resting in a semicircle above her blond head.

"Mona. Mona!"

Mona never slept really deeply. Almost at once she opened up her violet eyes in surprise, and then she sat up.

"I was asleep," she declared loudly and clearly.

"Have you seen Lars, Mona?"

Mona quizzically looked over at her brother's bed.

"Isn't he somewhere in the bed?"

"No. He must have gotten up, and we can't find him. Have you seen or heard anything of him?"

Mona shook her head slowly and seriously.

"No."

More or less as an afterthought, she said, "No. I was asleep."

Then she lay down, looked first at Jenny and then at her mother, back again at Jenny, and stated her concluding thought clearly.

"Now I am going to go back to sleep again."

Which she did.

Jenny's and Mrs. Tornquist's eyes met above the white bed. In spite of their concern they had to smile. Jenny went over to the closet and began poking around among the clothes there. A ball bat fell out with a thunderous thud.

"Is it possible that he went to the bathroom and fell asleep there? Lars can sleep absolutely anywhere."

"I've looked everywhere. In the big bathroom and both

small ones, and down in the kitchen. And the storm door is shut."

Jenny noticed that her mother's voice shook at the last words. She felt that she must pull herself together. Now she was wide awake.

"But that's impossible," she said resolutely. "He can't just have gone up in smoke. Let's look some more now. Really look."

They really searched. Shaking with cold, they went systematically through all the attic corners and the closets. They looked under beds and sofas and chairs. They called his name so many times that Viveca finally awakened. She had some new suggestions. "Try the linen closet and under the cellar stairs."

At length they were all three standing in the hall. They looked at each other almost as if to seek consolation in each other's eyes.

"He just isn't anywhere in the house," Viveca said positively.

"But the kitchen door is bolted from inside, and the storm door is locked. He can't have gotten out," said Jenny.

"The window!" cried Mrs. Tornquist. Suddenly her face became several shades whiter.

Jenny ran up the stairs again, for what seemed the umpteenth time—and soon returned to tell them that all the windows were shut and locked.

At that point her mother sank down into an easy chair with her arms hanging down at her sides. Viveca stood leaning against the opposite wall. From down by the road they could hear the rhythmic noise of a snow plow. Viveca, who for once in her life appeared with hair disheveled, remarked that the roads must be covered with snow again, a fact obvious to anyone who had even glanced out the windows in the last half hour.

"I'm standing here thinking about something," Jenny suddenly remarked. "Could he have gone out anyway, and then could the door have shut itself and locked again, the safety lock, I mean?"

She rushed over to the storm door. Her trembling hands fumbled with the doorknob. Both Viveca and her mother tried to help her. They had gotten a new spurt of energy.

The door opened out toward the gable.

What they saw at first was not encouraging. The ground was covered with a heavy white blanket of snow. A weak searchlight—how far away they couldn't tell—was the only break in the monotonous whiteness. Maybe it was just the old, familiar street lamps.

Jenny's feet, protected only by her slippers, sank deep into the wet snow on the front steps. They all three stared, trying to see through the curtain of snow, to make out details.

"Lars!" Mrs. Tornquist cried out. "La-a-a-ars, La-a-a-ars," echoed Jenny and Viveca. The wind blew the snow around them, far into the hall.

For a couple of seconds the snow glistened.

Almost at the same moment the three of them caught sight of something dark just a few yards away down toward the edge of the yard. A sled! And not only a sled.

Movement . . . something flying up the steps toward them . . .

"Mama! Ma-a-a-a-a -ha- m-a-a-a."

"Lars, Lars! *Where* have you been, Lars, honey?"

"Ma-a-a-ma! It was so da-a-a-a-ark, and it was snowing so hard."

"Lars, what in the world were you thinking about? How long have you been sitting out there?"

"Shut the door, Viveca! Otherwise we'll have snowdrifts all over the floor."

The doors were closed. Only the snow and the darkness remained outside.

Lars sat on a chair in the kitchen. The melting snow streamed out of his hair and down his face, neck, and throat. His mother began removing his comical, complicated clothing—consisting of his pajama jacket, a heavy turtle-neck sweater, ski pants, and felt slippers, thoroughly wet all of them. Viveca stood over by the stove, warming milk to make four cups of hot chocolate. Her blond hair, once more combed in pageboy style, was like a glistening helmet over her head.

"Now, Lars," Mrs. Tornquist said. "Now you've got to tell us. Why on earth did you go out, and how long were you sitting out there on the sled?"

Lars's eyes wandered aimlessly around the ceiling.

"Oh, many, many, many hours. The whole night."

"But you went to bed yesterday evening."

"Aw, he's just fibbing. He's never been able to tell the difference between seconds and minutes and hours."

The latter came from Viveca who was watching to see that the milk didn't boil over.

"Tell us now, Lars."

"O.K., O.K. Take it easy. I'm *going* to tell you."

Lars resembled an orator who had a captive audience before him. He began.

"Of course you heard the news yesterday evening about those thieves who stole a whole lot of diamonds and gold and rubies. And the police said that anyone who could capture the thieves would receive a big reward—several million crowns."

"Not million, silly!"

"Yes it was. Thousands and millions. They made off with quite a haul, you see!" Lars looked around triumphantly. "And I heard all about it on the radio, and then I went to bed and I thought of a plan. It's just for reasons like this that we have 'The Secret Club.'

"And I thought," he said very quietly, mainly because of the importance of his news, "I thought that I would call the other members together and *do* something."

He looked around again, saw that he still had his audience in the palm of his hand, and continued. "We've built a platform high up in a tree down by the dairy, and every day all the fellows have to climb up and see if any messages have come.

"And so I sneaked up and wrote this message on a piece of paper: 'Big jewel robbery. Police helpless. Millions promised in reward. Meet at the usual place.'"

"That jewel robbery was down in southern Sweden—

way down in Malmö, silly," remarked Viveca in a very superior manner.

"Of course. That's why I'm worried, you see. You don't think the thieves are sitting around in Malmö just waiting for the police to come and get them, do you? They can hide their jewels any old place, and here in Nordvik—that's where I would try to hide them if I were the thieves—here there aren't any police except those guys down at the police station, and nothing much ever happens there."

No one in his audience interrupted this statement. Lars's voice grew louder.

"I couldn't get away earlier in the evening because the girls were running around all over the place in the upstairs hall with wet hair. So I just went to bed and kept on the watch."

Breaking off his narrative, Lars suddenly looked puzzled. "Maybe I slept for just a little, tiny while. Because all of a sudden it was completely quiet and dark everywhere. So you see then I got up and put on my clothes. And whenever you leave a message for the members of the 'Secret Club,' you have to be in disguise, so I put on my beard and the false nose that I got for my birthday, and I also pasted some excelsior on my eyebrows . . ."

"I certainly hope you didn't meet anyone out there," said Viveca, clearly horrified at the thought. She had forgotten all about the milk, which, of course, had to go and boil over at that moment.

Jenny sat quietly on a kitchen stool, resting her chin in her hands. She had soft blue eyes, in the depths of which you could always sense happiness, but the expression on her face now was serious and attentive. Lars regarded her with satisfaction but paid no attention to Viveca's statement. Sullenly Viveca wiped up the mess that the milk had made on the stove and began to stir in the chocolate. Lars went on.

"And then I put the message in my pocket and sneaked down the stairs while everybody was asleep."

"That was in the middle of the night, Lars," his mother said reproachfully. "I think you're out of your mind to go out like that. It was purely accidental that I woke up. I thought it felt chilly in the room and that perhaps I should turn the thermostat up a little higher. Then I went in to cover you up because you always kick all your covers off."

Lars pretended not to notice this interruption. The expressions "cover you up" and "kick all your covers off" sounded childish and not at all in keeping with his new self-appointed role—that of the helper of the law.

"Go on, Lars," said Jenny.

"I left the door open just a little bit, because I didn't have a key. And then I sneaked down to the ditch alongside the road and stayed there and took a good look around."

"For what, if I might ask?" said Viveca.

"You never know," Lars answered condescendingly. "It could be a *gang* of thieves, and they could have spies around. Don't you understand?"

"No. But did you see anything?"

"It was dark. Real, real dark outside. No stars, no moon, no anything. And I crept carefully, cautiously, along by the fence, behind the hedge, and nobody saw me."

Lars took a couple of big, deep swallows out of his mug of chocolate and sighed contentedly. Jenny handed him a slice of bread, which she had just buttered. Lars had a far-away look in his eyes.

"When I got down to the dairy, there was a car driving along very slowly. I lay there, not moving a muscle, right there by the mailbox under the trees, and I didn't dare even to breathe because I saw that it was a police car. The kind with lights on top. Then it stopped."

"Lars!" Now it was Mrs. Tornquist's turn to look horrified. "And you had that nose and the beard and all that stuff on."

This had no effect on Lars. He was truly in the middle of his story.

"They rolled down the window, and I heard one of them say, 'Something's moving there in among the trees.' And one of them—a constable—got out of the car, and he had a *revolver* in his hand, and he said, 'Who's there? Speak up!' But I just stayed there, quiet as a mouse, because the members of 'The Secret Club' always have to keep out of sight. Just imagine if they had found out about the members' secret mailbox in the tree."

Lars made deep, new inroads into the mug of chocolate, possibly to escape the doubtful eyes that were directed toward him.

"Lars is fibbing now," said Viveca, slowly and emphatically.

"Well, anyway, there *was* a car," Lars repeated. But this time there was no mention of the police. "Then quick as lightning I climbed up into the secret tree and put the message into the box."

"Did you see the police on the way home, too?" Viveca asked sarcastically.

"No, but something else happened. Something completely terrific, let me tell you.

"It had begun to be windy and it was snowing a little bit too. So I hurried. I wanted to get home. But of course I sneaked all the way. And on the hill where there is that path right beside the road, along came a horse. Not just any old horse, believe me. I think it was probably a ghost horse, because I saw it only for a second and then it disappeared again, and it had some peculiar things across its nose. There was some kind of band there, and it glowed in the dark."

"Lars!"

Three voices raised in protest managed to halt the flow of words. Mrs. Tornquist added, as she ran her fingers through Lars's tousled hair, "You don't need to embroider the story. It's exciting enough as is, Lars."

"But I saw the horse, I really did," Lars declared. His eyes became wide and dark. "It walked out onto the road right under the light, and it snorted and seemed to be enjoying itself."

"Perhaps it was an elk," Jenny suggested reassuringly. "I saw one down there last fall. An elk without horns."

Lars thought this over for a minute. He left the elk to its own destiny, more or less as he had the police.

"The last part of the way home I had to walk all bent

over because it was blowing so hard. And when I got home, I saw that the door had blown shut—locked, and everything."

"But why didn't you ring the bell?"

"I did. I rang and rang and rang. But nobody came."

"The bell is broken," Viveca said expressionlessly. "I noticed it yesterday evening." She looked anxiously at her watch, obviously thinking of her examination in Swedish.

"I knocked and I hollered too," Lars said in a voice that suddenly sounded pitiable and woebegone. "But nobody heard. Finally I got out the sled and sat on it. I took off the beard and the false nose because they felt so wet and nasty." He stuck his hands into the pockets of his pants, which were hung on a nearby chair to dry, and soberly took out two strange, unidentifiable objects. "Look. They are completely ruined. Yes, Mother, I sat there all night long."

"My poor dear," said Lars's mother as she pressed his wet head to her side. "Come upstairs and go to bed now. You can stay home from school and get over this adventure. And you must promise me that you'll never, never again go out like this."

Viveca's glance followed them as they disappeared through the kitchen door.

"Yeah," she said bitterly. "Look at him. He's in the first grade and he gets to stay home and rest. But I. I'm in the eleventh grade, and I have a four-hour examination in Swedish, and nobody cares about that!"

Frantically she rattled the dishes in the sink.

Jenny's arms hung loosely at her sides. Now that the excitement was over, she felt the tiredness and chill creeping through her and spreading to every part of her body.

"It's six o'clock," she said. "I'm going to get dressed and go to the stable."

This remark really didn't call for an answer, and the only thing to be heard was a contemptuous snort from Viveca.

CHAPTER 7

Setbacks

Jenny would long remember the morning after Lars's nocturnal mission for The Secret Club for two reasons. For one thing, it was the first time she experienced a strange feeling of dissatisfaction and disappointment after riding Rascal. She knew, of course, that dispiritedness and tiredness were invariably communicated from rider to horse and that it was the fault of the rider if they couldn't manage to overcome these factors together. It was natural that the excitement she had been through and the fatigue that sometimes overcame her should leave their mark on Rascal. But in any case, Jenny couldn't rid herself of a feeling of surprise over Rascal's behavior. She had gradually come to regard Rascal as the perfect, even-tempered horse, never tired, never contrary, always prepared to cooperate with her rider in achieving a happy feeling of mutual accomplishment. But on that raw, forbidding morning, Rascal had not only behaved peculiarly, but also, once or twice, had seemed just plain nervous.

Perhaps, Jenny thought, Rascal's behavior might be traceable to the biting gusts of wind blowing in from the sea. The darkness was oppressive. It was the end of November, and even if Jenny stuck to the well-lighted paths and roads, both horse and rider could feel the heavy grip of winter for the first time.

Knowing that she hadn't been quite herself that morning, Jenny gave Rascal a consolation prize of an extra portion of hard bread and two sugar lumps. With special care she cleaned the elegant, small hoofs, which had had to walk in so much snow and slush that morning.

Because she had taken a little extra time with Rascal, she arrived five minutes late for her first class and found, to her horror, that the classroom was empty. For some reason the lesson was obviously being given in some other room. But why? And where, in the huge, complicated school building? Jenny was at a loss; she stood, ill at ease, in the empty corridor. She felt desolate and left out—a sensation that was heightened by her being able to hear the old, familiar murmur from the nearby classrooms. For no apparent reason, a couple of lines from a poem that they had recently read in class began to spin around in Jenny's head—a phenomenon that had happened to her time and time again of late, sometimes in the most ridiculous connection.

"Terror gripped the cherubim.

To God their flight advanced . . ."

Jenny had to smile to herself. She looked up and down the corridors. Where would she begin to search for the class?

"Terror gripped . . ."

It was then that the other thing happened that was to make that mixed-up morning memorable.

She heard steps on the stairs. They approached along the

corridor, quickly, forcefully. Jenny thought it would be a teacher and, sighing deeply, she steeled herself against the inevitable inquisition and the long drawn-out explanation that would have to follow.

Her second sigh was one of relief. Jenny saw that it was only Kristofer, the owner of Ramrod, whom she often met on her rides through the Nordvik woods.

"Hi, there. What are you doing here?" said Kristofer in amazement.

"My class has disappeared," Jenny explained. "I came late, and now there's no class."

Kristofer looked in through the wide open door of the classroom. But he immediately returned his attention to Jenny. He thought she seemed much smaller and more helpless out here in the corridor than she did on the back of a horse. She had on a small gray knitted sweater that fitted well, but her beige jodhpurs, with the leather patches on the insides of the knees, were wrinkled all the way down her legs. They had been an expensive purchase, and they were big enough so that she would be able to grow into them.

As he looked at her, Kristofer began to think of a deserted elephant baby who hadn't yet grown sufficiently to fill his skin. He began to feel a little self-conscious about his age and his own size, and he said, "Listen, you're a member of the Nordvik Riding Club, aren't you?"

"Yes, since last week," said Jenny, stretching herself up to a height sufficient to banish most of the wrinkles in the jodhpur legs.

"That's good. We're going to ride through Nordvik

again this year in the parade on Lucia Day. You know, in a big, long line from the stables to the castle. Do you want to join us? You're pretty much at home in the saddle."

"That certainly would be a lot of fun," said Jenny. Her heart was beating extra hard, and blood rushed to her cheeks, all the way up to her smooth, dark hairline. "We'll have to carry torches too, won't we?"

"Yes, sure. But that's nothing as long as you have a calm horse with the disposition of a camel. I'm going to ride

Beauty. She's great, once you get used to her. Look, we'll ride the path some evening for practice, and I'll tell you more about the parade later on."

"Very polite of you," Jenny murmured, fastening her eyes on Kristofer's tie. The past couple of years she had suddenly begun having attacks of being unprepared, of knowing neither what she was going to say nor where to look. However, she had already learned a remedy. You merely grasped hold of reality and held fast to it. At this moment reality was her class, which had disappeared.

"Almost a fourth of the period has gone," she said. "Where shall I go?"

"What subject do you have?" asked Kristofer, being utterly practical. He ran his fingers through his coarse blond hair—a sure sign that he intended to tackle the problem in a scientific fashion.

"Composition, with the Navy woman."

They glanced at each other, saying nothing more, but each understanding. The teacher in composition was active in the Women's Naval Reserve—a fact that she would never let her pupils forget. Kristofer had also had her as a teacher.

"I know!" he said suddenly. "Some character is here from Oxford. He gave a lecture for the upper classmen yesterday—with slides—down in the auditorium. Run down and look. Matter of fact, I am going in that direction. I'll come along with you."

They rushed through the corridor and down the steps. A janitor gave them a suspicious glance, but Kristofer, his eyes straight ahead, and an untroubled grin on his face, looked straight through him.

With utmost caution they opened the heavy door to the auditorium. Waves of perfect Oxford English floated out from the darkness.

Kristofer pushed Jenny in toward the back row.

"Sneak in and sit down," he whispered. "Nobody will notice you."

CHAPTER 8

Transactions in the Stable

In Sweden, where the winters are long and the days, during December, are very short, the Christmas season really starts on the thirteenth of December, St. Lucia Day. The fairest-haired girl in a household, a village, or a particular group is chosen to be Lucia. In the early hours of the morning, or in the evening instead, she appears dressed in white, wearing a crown of lighted candles in her hair, symbolic of the coming of light. Accompanied by attendants in white and by Star Boys, also in white costumes and tall, pointed hats, she serves coffee and special wheat cookies to all.

That year Nordvik experienced a real Lucia festival. Biting cold and snowdrifts had come on schedule. Nordvik Bay was frozen over completely, and it was wonderful to watch the icy arrowheads of the stars gleaming down on some of the clear evenings. A couple of snowstorms, bringing with them the raw cold straight from the Arctic Ocean, had played havoc with traffic on the streets and on the small coastal road. But storm or no storm, the calendar moved ahead irrevocably.

On the thirteenth of December Jenny woke up with the frightening knowledge that the autumn term had simply slipped away, in spite of the fact that she herself felt it had barely begun. She lay still for several minutes, aware of the darkness and gloom hanging over her like black, predatory birds, but then, as she remembered what day it was, her thoughts grew warm and lighthearted and wandered to Rascal.

In a moment the darkness literally disappeared. Mona came in, dressed as Lucia, with a crown of candles in her hair, followed by Lars, who had livened up his pure white Star Boy's costume with a newly purchased beard and wild, bushy eyebrows.

The stable had its own Lucia ceremony an hour later. There Jenny, in the saddle, with Rascal well groomed and shiny, played the part of the Star Boy. Gunilla, riding the thoroughbred Saba, was in the place of honor as Lucia with a brilliant wreath of electric lights in her hair. She rode sidesaddle, and the folds of her white gown against Saba's gleaming, black body lent an almost medieval touch to the scene.

Gunilla had light brown hair and a fair complexion, but in spite of the fact that she rode well, Jenny could not help thinking what a really wonderful Lucia Mariann would have been with her almost white-blond hair and her serious face. She would not have smiled uneasily in the direction of the grandstand, fearful of not measuring up, as Gunilla did continually. She would have been the center of attention as Lucia, but she would have devoted herself entirely to the business of riding Saba. In vain, Jenny searched the faces of the crowd up there in the stands. She realized at last that Mariann who, under different circumstances, would almost surely have led the procession around the ring, didn't want to join the spectators on such a day.

Jenny had arrived a few minutes late and had had to devote her time to Rascal right up to the moment she was to take her place in the procession with the other Star Boy riders. She therefore wasn't aware of the absence of the riding instructor until they were already walking in a circle around the ring.

Just at that moment there was a movement at the entrance to the ring. As a shrill voice called out words of command, the usual crowd of small boys, most of them Lars's age, disappeared in haste like a school of small fish, and right after that Manilla made her entrance—an entrance so astonishing that the whole troop moving around the edge of the ring stopped automatically. Everyone was dumfounded.

As usual, Manilla had been left over after everyone had chosen his horse. She was just too old and slow to compete with the more attractive mounts. But now she was literally stumbling into the ring, carrying on her sway back a rider the like of whom had never been seen within the venerable walls of the stables.

He was a tall man with a long face and fairly long hair. Everything about him seemed elongated in some peculiar fashion, a fact that was only emphasized by his astonishing riding outfit: a bright red coat, riding pants that fitted better than any Jenny had ever seen, black jockey cap, and shiny, black boots.

It was pretty obvious that he had used a whip on the surprised and shocked Manilla. Possibly he had even launched some sort of attack on the two Scotties who, because of the rigid discipline of the stables, never stuck their noses into the arena area. Plainly everything was in a state of disorder now, and both Scotties were running around in the tanbark as if they had lost their minds.

With no small effort Jenny regained her power of speech.

"Where's our regular riding instructor?" she asked of a friend nearby.

"He has the flu. This must be the riding instructor who is going to substitute. They borrowed him from Surby, I heard."

Jenny had to suppress a strong desire to roar with laughter. The Scotties had disappeared with legs flying, but Manilla was still standing in the middle of the ring. She was phlegmatic and passive by nature, and many Nordvik children had had their first ride on her back. But she was not exactly a thing of beauty with her elongated body and her sway back. Now she looked not only stupid but also completely unstrung. The whip lash and the tight reins had confused her completely. The contrast between the horse and the elegant man in the saddle created a strange and comical effect.

The whole riding academy stared. A feeling of stupefied amazement spread from the ring to the grandstands, infecting the otherwise joyful spectators. Gunilla forgot that as Lucia she should have been the center of attention. She sank down in the saddle and stared, mouth agape, just like everyone else.

Unfortunately, the substitute riding instructor didn't understand the situation. He decided, with growing self-

confidence, that he had skillfully commanded respect from the first moment, and he tightened the reins still more.

"Form a procession," he yelled. "Straighten your back, Lucia."

For the next few seconds Jenny could see the whites of Manilla's eyes. She caught Kristofer's glance diagonally across the ring. His Star Boy hat added at least half a yard to his already considerable height. To give some vent to his feelings he was looking cross-eyed.

Jenny shook with inward laughter. Of course, they had learned the introductory turns of the quadrille almost to perfection, and the morning's performance under the direction of the regular riding instructor would have been a trouble-free and happy event for all concerned. But now everything had been changed into a barracks exercise. The bewildered Manilla scampered ceaselessly back and forth across the ring, with her peculiarly dressed rider shouting wild commands.

Jenny could barely hold Rascal's reins. Everyone was quite accustomed to riding, so there were no accidents, but the quadrille ended in general confusion. Some of the riders lay across their horses' necks, half choked with laughter, while some, wearing serious expressions on their faces, did just the opposite of all the commands. The gallery soon caught onto it, and they shouted wildly. It was a lucky thing for the riding instructor that the whole show had been late in getting under way and that it now had to come to an end so that everybody could get to school on time for the Lucia festival there.

Once back in the stalls the mood was quieter. The horses

were anxious to get to their well-filled cribs, and Bengt passed around a tray with hot spiced wine, called glögg, for all the participants. The friendly shadows under the roof beams, the sounds of contented munching from the stalls, and the warm drinks worked together to calm the riders' high spirits. The riding instructor stood alone with his glögg glass. Here and there you could still hear a giggle over his performance on Manilla, but pretty soon things quieted down. The riders were making ready for the next chapter in the story of Lucia Day.

Just then Jenny saw the new riding instructor raise his hand and point, with a dictatorial gesture, toward Rascal's stall.

"Everyone who is to take part in the Lucia Procession must meet here in the riding academy at seven o'clock. And I want that horse to be reserved for my use." Turning to Bengt, he continued, "See to it that he's taken care of and saddled in good time."

Jenny opened her mouth to say something, but she found no words. She looked helplessly at Bengt, who was sullenly looking the riding instructor up and down.

"That isn't a *he*," he said contemptuously. "It's a *she*, and she is privately owned."

"Privately owned!" repeated the riding master as if it were the first time he had ever heard these words. "Who owns her, anyway?"

Bengt pointed with his thumb at Jenny, who hastily turned her head the other way and pretended to be completely occupied with tickling the stable cat under the chin.

"That girl over there," he said morosely.

Jenny looked back at Bengt appreciatively, but he didn't return the compliment.

"That nasty riding instructor," Jenny mumbled to the cat. "Why did he pick on Rascal? The stables are full of horses."

For a moment the riding instructor looked as if he intended to launch a direct attack against Jenny. But good sense won out. He turned his attention elsewhere, and this time, unfortunately, his eyes fell on Beauty.

"Then I will take that one," he announced.

But the good fairy was at Kristofer's side too. For the second time that morning Jenny saw him look cross-eyed, this time at Bengt.

"Beauty is also, ummmh, private," said Kristofer in a reverent tone of voice. A large guffaw echoed throughout the stalls. Some of the riders near him took a deep swallow out of their glögg glasses. Mariann would have died at the thoughts of this strange riding instructor on her favorite horse, Jenny reflected.

"Palma belongs to the academy, and she is a fine horse," Bengt suggested quickly.

During the tense silence that followed, the riding instructor inspected Palma and finally indicated his decision by means of a curt nod. In the age-old manner he flourished his whip against his elegant boots, unaware that a dozen youngsters with experienced eyes were observing and classifying him: a weak man trying to imitate a strong one.

Jenny took a couple of steps in Bengt's direction. He hadn't been at all friendly toward her of late, but had seemed strange and bitter instead. Perhaps things would be all right again now.

"Thanks for saving Rascal for me," she said, behaving as she usually did toward people she was fond of—warmly, nicely. "That riding instructor is such a swollen toad that he makes you lose your power of speech."

Even before her words had died away she knew that she might as well have been talking to the walls. Bengt didn't as much as look at her. He stared out into space and said, "Oh, well, it probably isn't much fun to be a grown man and a riding instructor and everything and have to ride Manilla, while some little snip of a girl is sitting on the stable's finest, most elegant horse."

Jenny's smile collapsed just like a Venetian blind at a window. So *that* was the trouble! Bengt was jealous because she owned Rascal. To her own surprise, Jenny discovered that she had within her a volcano of mounting exasperation.

"You think you're real tough, don't you?" she said. "Well, Rascal is mine, I want you to know, and it doesn't concern you or anybody else."

Jenny's heart beat wildly. She didn't look at Bengt again but turned around and walked away. But even halfway to school she noticed that she was violently hitting her gloves against each other.

CHAPTER 9

The Lucia Parade

"It's fun to hear a small girl roar like a lion," said a voice from a stall on the other side of the stable.

Jenny jumped and looked up from Rascal's saddle girth, which she was smoothing. Her cheeks reddened. She hadn't been aware that anyone had been a witness to the encounter between her and Bengt.

"The lion—or perhaps I should say lioness—was completely in the right. Blame it on our national fault—Royal Swedish Envy."

Kristofer stepped forward out of the shadows and stood right under the roof light. He had on a ceremonial white fur coat and looked so huge and military that Jenny once again felt the old uncertainty mounting and her face becoming bright red. But then as she saw the gleeful laughter in his eyes, everything was fine again.

"Do you think so?" she said, relieved. "I wondered . . . I thought perhaps I had behaved badly. Mariann would have had much more self-control. There's no getting around the fact that Bengt doesn't have his own horse, and he really plugs away and works very hard."

"Everybody can't have a horse like Rascal," said Kristofer generously. "And if you had loaned her to the riding instructor, I would have shot you and Rascal both."

They laughed together, and Jenny resumed her work on the saddle.

"That's a really elegant fur coat you've got," she said appreciatively.

"Glad you like it," Kristofer replied. "It belongs to the gym teacher; I borrowed it. Every white fur coat in Nordvik will be on display this evening. Of course, the riding instructor has his own and he looks just adorable in it." Kristofer made the latter statement in a high-pitched, girlish voice.

But Jenny's thoughts were dwelling, for the moment, on more serious things. She ran her hands along Rascal's withers.

"Can you come here a minute and look?" she asked him, her voice lowered.

Kristofer came over.

"What do you want me to look at?"

"At Rascal, naturally."

"I'll be glad to do that just any old time, especially when you're riding her."

Jenny looked long and seriously at Kristofer. These sudden changes in his conversation, coupled with his ability at repartee, made her certain that he was much more interesting than ordinary boys. At the same time, strangely enough, his out-of-the-way and unexpected behavior inspired confidence. Jenny couldn't fathom the combination.

But she didn't lose her train of thought.

"That's not what I meant. Look, it's just that she hasn't really been herself these last few weeks. Now today I didn't notice anything special. But sometimes, when I take her out in the mornings, she seems listless—somehow tired."

Kristofer had come all the way into the stall, and he stood, with his hands stuffed in the pockets of the fine white fur coat, observing Rascal. He didn't say anything, but he was such a good listener that Jenny was encouraged to continue.

"In the beginning she was happy and frisky. You know, I can swear that when I wanted to gallop, she wanted to too, and when I wanted to walk her, it was as if she sensed this intuitively. Perhaps, simply because everything was so new and wonderful last fall, my memory is hazy, and maybe I'm only imagining things. But a couple of times recently I actually had to force her to do what I wanted. It seems sometimes that the only thing she wants is to get back to the stable. Do you know what I mean?"

Kristofer walked slowly around Rascal. He felt her knees and hocks tenderly and lifted and inspected her hoofs. Her three white "stockings" were in sharp contrast to the shadows in the stall.

He whistled softly to himself.

"Of course you check to see that everything is as it should be before you take her out, don't you?" he asked. "That nothing rubs her, that the girth isn't too loose, the halter isn't twisted, and all that sort of thing?"

"Naturally. I'm extra special careful now that I feel there's something that isn't quite right. Do you think she could be unhappy or sad here? That she's homesick for Vernestad, I mean?"

Jenny looked anxiously at Kristofer. The tow-headed boy shook his head.

"I thought you said she seemed contented and that everything was O.K. in the beginning, didn't you?"

"Yes. Yes, it was."

"Hmmm. Have you said anything to the riding instructor about all this? He knows everything there is to know about horses."

"Yes, I did. He examined her all over and said that nothing was wrong anywhere. And at that time the veterinarian was here on a routine visit, you see, and he said that she was in the finest possible condition."

"Well, then, I guess you're getting all hot and bothered over nothing. Of course, this is your first horse, and you feel very responsible and all that. It's probably nothing."

"But there's something else, too, Kristofer." Jenny's voice sank. "I couldn't tell the riding instructor, you see. Just little things, but still . . .

"One morning when I came the saddle was hanging backwards up there on the wall." Jenny pointed to it. "I'd swear that I've never hung it that way myself. And then there was the business with the left front hoof. I *know* that I cleaned all the hoofs well the day before because we had been on a long ride—it was a Sunday. I remember it especially well because there was lots of frost and snow, and a lot of stuff had gotten stuck on and frozen fast. The riding instructor showed me how to use a hoof pick to get the obstructions out. And then the next morning, when I looked at her hoofs, I found that the left front one had not really been cleaned."

Jenny looked up at Kristofer, who slowly rubbed his chin. Behind them at the stable entrance they heard the tramp of hoofs, accompanied by the sound of happy, excited voices. It was almost seven o'clock.

"That does sound peculiar," Kristofer said. He was not the type who hurried when he had a problem to figure out, but Jenny glanced uneasily at her watch. "Perhaps you cleaned one of the front hoofs twice and forgot the other one the day before. That can happen if you are interrupted, can't it?"

But Jenny shook her head.

"Not the way that hoof looked! Do you believe . . ." Her voice sank to a whisper. "It probably isn't possible, but do you suppose that someone might be borrowing her and riding her on the sly?"

They looked at each other straight across Rascal's nose. Kristofer seemed preoccupied.

At that moment they heard a shrill, dictatorial voice coming from the top of the stable hill. Kristofer made a face.

"I agree. It sounds peculiar. Gee, Rascal is a pretty thing. Her head is so wonderful, and her eyes are so wide set."

"Is Beauty saddled and ready?" Jenny asked anxiously. The commotion around them had begun to die down. Suddenly Bengt came into view with a broom in his hands.

"Still standing here? Are you completely out of your minds? The procession starts soon!" His expression was as sour as it had been that morning. Jenny pretended not to see him. She took Rascal by the reins.

At the gateway, Kristofer and Beauty caught up with them. Together they stepped outside from the twilight of the stall, with its special smell and its silence, into the liveliness of the midwinter evening.

A couple of the horses neighed, perhaps as a greeting for Beauty and Rascal, perhaps from pure joy at being out under the stars and in the cold—not bitter, but the sort that felt good and fresh and smooth against your cheeks. From the gables of the stable shone strong electric lamps, which lighted up both the roads leading into the town. The stable yard, triangular in shape, was usually half dark and quiet, but now it was aglow with newly fallen snow and with the flames from some of the torches, which had already been lighted. The edge of the woods stood out black as pitch on the other side of the railroad, and high in the sky, resting peacefully, was a lazy, bright crescent moon.

"That's a new moon," remarked Kristofer, who was already in the saddle.

Rascal pricked up her ears. As Jenny petted her, she thought, with satisfaction, that they were really in tune with one another this evening. She lighted her torch from Kristofer's. The dancing flames leaped up at once. Previously they had had instruction in riding with torches, and neither Rascal nor Beauty had blinked an eye at these innovations that their beloved but unpredictable riders had introduced. Rascal still had some of the warm air from the stall in her lungs, and the breath escaping from her nostrils came out in fine white pillows.

As they looked down the road leading to the stables, they suddenly sighted Lucia's glistening crown. All the riders craned their necks. The Lucia selected for this year was a nineteen-year-old girl who worked every day in a grocery store. She was small and blond and almost completely hidden by her large white fur coat. She was to lead the procession in the academy's own green and silver sleigh, which was to be drawn by two big ponies that had been borrowed for the occasion from a riding academy in a neighboring town.

The substitute riding instructor kept popping up among the horses and riders, full of meddlesome eagerness. He gave and took back so many commands that the procession would surely have been late if the participants had not been firmly disciplined, and if they hadn't been trained in the processional and recessional under the direction of their own riding instructor.

With Kristofer in the saddle, Beauty disappeared in the darkness toward the group that was to be in the lead. Jenny, on Rascal, took her place among the rear guard alongside a classmate who was riding a beautiful, cream-colored mare. This girl, whose name was Ingrid, was sure in the saddle, and her horse Pique was known as one of the most trustworthy in the stable. Rascal and Pique liked being teamed together. Ingrid and Jenny exchanged similar opinions as to the riding instructor's behavior.

Then suddenly, quietly, and with no fuss, just as the old stable clock struck its seven thunderous tones, the procession started. The torches of the riders in the lead could be seen shining brightly down by the railroad. Both of the ponies drawing Lucia's sleigh walked with lowered heads as if they were out on a heavy, serious everyday mission, but everything else actually seemed to glide along easily, smoothly, unhesitatingly through the snow. Lucia looked fragile, ethereal, and terribly pale. She had never before been in the limelight, and in addition she was afraid, not only of the sound of the horses' hoofs, but also of the sparks from the torches, which seemed to swarm, like fireflies, in the darkness around her and which sometimes cascaded over her and the sleigh.

Right behind Lucia came two sleighs carrying the four attendants, of whom Viveca was one. Then came the riding instructor on Palma. He made use of spurs—which Palma wasn't used to—but since she was a peaceful, well-trained horse, she gave him no trouble.

For the people of Nordvik, who in general were not riders themselves, the Lucia Procession was a dazzling drama. The roads, which were usually choked every day with delivery trucks, motorcycles, motor scooters, private cars, and huge oil trucks, looked as if time had gone back a hundred years, and the town had an old-fashioned story-book quality about it. For a change all the noisy motors were stifled. For once everyone discovered just how silent it could be in the quietude of a snow-clad winter evening. You felt as if you wanted to sink down into the snow, stretch out in it, and come out rested. The merry noise of the bells on the ponies spread like quicksilver throughout Nordvik, alerting the crowd to the arrival of the procession. The longer the bells sounded, the more crowded with spectators the routes became.

Nordvik was a small town, and seldom was an event of sufficient interest to cause the whole town's population to assemble. Now the townspeople had caught the spirit of the festivities, and as they crowded along the streets, they grew noisier when they noticed how their voices echoed in the stillness.

The procession continued down toward the center of town. Greetings were exchanged, and the inevitable gatherings of boys of ten or twelve began to make their presence known by means of some illegally acquired firecrackers.

But Lucia's ponies walked independently and purposefully on, and the alert troops of riders maintained their disciplined calmness. The only person who seemed to be irritated was the riding instructor who, to the delight of the boys, shouted a few swear words as the spectacle moved on.

The academy's horses and their young riders—averaging about fifteen years of age—made a magnificent showing throughout the whole town. Lucia overcame her shyness as she entered into the festive mood, which spread as the parade approached the town's center. She waved and smiled and forgot the horses' hoofs and the sparks from the torches. But still it couldn't be helped: the heroine of the day came out second best when compared with the well-dressed riders surrounding her.

The route led over the hill where the school was located and down through the valley separating it from the castle heights. Here lay the city's oldest quarter with its small red cottages, at one time the dwelling places of those who served the lords of the mighty manors. The cottages nestled modestly in the shadow of the massive walls of the castle. On this slope above them, spring would shyly present her first snowdrops or crocuses and, a little later, anemones, just as modestly as if they had been casually constructed and thrown there by elves and fairies. But now the heaviness of winter lay over the slope. The glow of the torchlight procession flickered on the ice-covered cliffs.

In the courtyard of the fourteenth century castle standing torches blazed. Here, where the families and the elderly citizens had congregated to enjoy the sight of the approaching procession from the winding street down in the valley and to witness the climax of the evening—Lucia's arrival and subsequent coronation on the castle steps, the songs of her attendants, and music by the school band—the crowd was tremendous. The band was already blaring loudly.

At the foot of the castle hill the members of the procession received new torches. The riders in the lead had already reached the edge of the castle courtyard. The feeling of jubilation among the people, who had been biding their time patiently but expectantly, started swelling and growing. The brass band played "The Finnish Rider's March" as a salute to the main body of the parade.

Jenny noticed that Rascal was prancing. She knew that some of the spectators had given her a good bit of flattering attention as she came by on her horse, but she was surprised that Rascal could feel it too and act accordingly. Rascal held her head high, and it glistened in the light from the torches. She also lifted her feet higher than usual.

Slowly Lucia's sleigh moved through the crowd. The two ponies worked dutifully and didn't attempt to show off as the finer riding horses had begun to do. The riders in the lead had separated, moved up, and stationed themselves at the steps.

The members of the riding club had been trained properly in their duties, but they had guessed wrongly on two counts: the number of people who would be there to watch and the ability of the police force to hold them at a distance. For the riders in the lead, everything went according to schedule, but when the sleighs arrived in front of the castle steps, the people began to crowd forward. Curious onlookers, many of whom had already seen the procession down below, stormed up the many small paths of the castle heights. Children who, from the beginning of time, it would seem, knew every single path on the hill, used these paths also and appeared in droves. They rushed in between the side buildings and from around the corners of the castle. In snake-dance fashion they forced themselves into the crowd, each one convinced that he or she didn't take up much room at all, completely confident of being able to worm his or her way through to the center of events. The crowd swelled in the area between the castle and its wings, the isolated policemen resembled currants hidden in a fruit cake, and the band found, to its amazement, that it no longer had the leading role. The riding instructor added to the confusion by giving contradictory commands.

The space in front of Lucia, where the rear guard was to have assembled in a semicircle, was suddenly crawling with noisy, screaming small boys. Suddenly—whether by accident or on purpose, no one ever knew—a firecracker exploded in the middle of the crowd. Jenny saw Paulette rear up. Her teammate in the lead, a dapple gray, was shoved from the rear, and she laid back her ears and began to lash her tail back and forth. However, the boy riding her was equal to the situation. He petted the horse's neck and talked calmly, consolingly to her.

Rascal and Pique behaved in an exemplary fashion. Jenny and Ingrid managed to hold them as the tumult began. The horses remained side by side, drawing warmth and comfort from each other. Rascal pricked up her ears.

Jenny rose in the stirrups in an attempt to get a broader view and to decide how she and Ingrid would best be able to get up to their positions beside Lucia's sleigh. She saw the gray kick and noticed Paulette against the wall of the wing, looking very mischievous indeed. As a matter of fact, she could see only a small fraction of the castle courtyard, but she had an idea that the rear guard had separated. She wondered if it were she herself or Rascal who was most responsible for the calm that prevailed around them. An older man with military bearing had said a couple of appreciative things about Rascal and Pique. He had a thunderous voice, which could be heard far and wide. Jenny blushed as she curtsied in the saddle.

She turned to Ingrid.

"Do you think it would be best if we tried to get up there with the leaders? They are in their right places, I can see, and up there on the castle road there aren't so many people. At least there weren't when I last looked."

Ingrid nodded.

"We could ride around the wing," she suggested. "Out in the courtyard there's too much going on."

The shrill, desperate blast of a police whistle sounded. The crowds only became worse and worse. The fluttering lights from the wavering torches bounced around among horses and spectators.

Jenny and Ingrid succeeded in getting their horses onto a narrow strip of ground near the wall of the wing where the crowd had thinned out. Following Ingrid's suggestion, they rode around the corner, and continued on around the back part of the wing, where there was hardly any crowd at all. They emerged between the wall and a gable of the castle and found that it was just as Jenny had predicted. The riders who had been in the lead stood together, apparently undisturbed, at their posts. Jenny and Ingrid rode up in back of them. They found a vantage point—in reality a flower bed that had been lovingly tended and manicured by the municipal gardener—and were finally able to see what was going on.

"It's just as you'd imagine," Ingrid said angrily. "If only that stupid instructor had taken it easy and hadn't gone here and there with his silly commands, everything would have been all right, even though it might have taken a little time."

Jenny nodded in agreement.

The rider in front of them turned his head.

"You said it!" Jenny recognized the voice as Kristofer's. "If only the rear guard had stood still and done nothing themselves until the people got quiet and took their places, everything would have gone as it should have. All of the horses are under control. But then that riding instructor had to begin riding back and forth, directing them first to the right and then to the left, and now everything is complete chaos. Listen to him carrying on."

"Wouldn't it be marvelous if Palma lost her good temper and threw him off," Jenny mused.

"At least we haven't had any accidents," observed Kristofer. "And it's all due to our own riding instructor and his well-trained pupils! But look. This man doesn't even begin to understand. He thinks everything is going all right because of him. Just look!"

It was quite obvious that the riding instructor was enjoying the role of leader. His shrill voice rose above the crowd.

"Quiet here. Quiet, everybody. Ride up to the right."

The band leader started to give the downbeat, but immediately the riding instructor rode up to him.

"Stop, now, until further notice. Let up for a while. You might frighten the horses with your noise."

Kristofer and Beauty snorted in chorus.

"Stupid dope," Kristofer said between his teeth.

The expression on the band leader's face, when the riding instructor classified his well-rehearsed music as "noise," was hard to describe. But he lowered his baton.

Peace and quiet began to return.

Lucia and her attendants had experienced some bad moments among the prancing horses in the flaming torchlight. Out of curiosity Jenny looked down at the sleigh and caught sight of Viveca, who was quite pale and who looked, for once, as if she had lost her poise. Jenny thought how lucky it was that none of the ponies who were pulling the sleighs had taken fright at the turn of events.

Lucia herself, all white and blond under the shimmering wreaths of lights, prepared to get out of the sleigh. The riding instructor had succeeded in making his way over to her, and he gave her a snappy salute.

The band leader again raised his baton, and on his face was the studied expression of great patience.

CHAPTER 10

Rascal on Her Own

Then it happened.

Jenny had been concentrating her entire attention on what was transpiring around Lucia. Especially she had concentrated on Viveca to see how she was going to carry out her duties, and to find something, if possible, that she could later tease her sister about. Therefore, when Rascal lurched suddenly, it came as a complete surprise to Jenny.

For several seconds, until she began to understand just what was happening, she was utterly bewildered, and those seconds turned out to be fateful. Rascal threw her head back and walked several steps alongside Beauty, shoving Palma from the rear on the way by, just at the moment when Palma and the riding instructor were the center of everyone's attention at the Lucia sleigh. Palma was already unnerved both by the earlier confusion among the horses and by the substitute riding instructor's use of spurs. She reared up so high that you could see her front feet and one of her white "stockings" in the torchlight.

Jenny saw the tall, thin figure of the riding instructor, clad in the white fur coat and the tight breeches, fly grotesquely high into the air. She didn't see where and how

he fell, but she noticed that Palma took off with an empty saddle and bolted.

Afterwards she could also recall how Viveca got up, lost her balance, and toppled backwards into the attendants' sleigh. A couple of the horses, who saw their comrade bolting away, neighed wildly.

Jenny tugged on Rascal's reins with all her might. Rascal did slow down, but her ears were laid back angrily as she continued a few additional steps.

Just as suddenly as she had started, she stopped.

It was obvious to Jenny that Rascal was looking for something specific and that she was going about it firmly and systematically. Actually, she had moved only a few lengths from her position at the castle wall, in spite of the fact that the consequences of her move had been quite extensive.

Rascal halted in front of a group of young people. Jenny had noticed them in the last few minutes, partly because they were pretty noisy and partly because she had seen Kristofer sending humorous salutes to them. Now she recognized them. They were all students in Kristofer's grade, and Jenny knew that the boy who stood nearest—the one whose merry eyes were so alert and whose dark hair hung down over his forehead—was named Michael and that he often went around with Kristofer.

He was at least as tall as Kristofer, but he was thinner. The girl beside him scarcely came up to his shoulders. She was dressed in a bright red parka and gray ski pants. The hood of the jacket, trimmed in white, was hanging down her back. Her whole face lit up with laughter as Rascal unexpectedly appeared before them. She had glistening white teeth and blond hair, which she wore in a sleek page-boy style except for the small, straggling curls that appeared around her forehead.

As for Jenny, she blushed up to the roots of her hair. Like all the other girls in her class, Jenny was a great admirer of this particular girl, although at an appropriate distance. To be sure, this girl had been home with Viveca a couple of times, but on those occasions Viveca had carefully closed the door to her room after they had gone in.

The girl's name was Cecilia Acker, and Jenny admired everything about her—that she was so perfect in height, that she was so slender, that her voice was lower and more serious than you could have expected, that she nodded and smiled at Jenny so nicely whenever they met on the school grounds, even though she must have recognized hundreds of girls similarly, and, perhaps first and foremost, that Cecilia, so unaffected, free, and easy in her manner, was always in Michael's company.

Why, oh, why did Rascal behave so strangely and walk up to her in particular, making it appear that Jenny had no control over her horse?

And as if that in itself weren't sufficient, Rascal now stretched her head toward Cecilia, wrinkled her lips, and nuzzled against the side of Cecilia's jacket where there was a zipper pocket. There, on the beautiful red garment, Rascal left a trail of slobbers.

Jenny, seeking desperately for the right and proper thing to say, gave up trying and abandoned herself to becoming more and more embarrassed.

Cecilia looked a bit puzzled and even a little apprehensive, but Michael shook with laughter.

"Cecilia," he said. "Cecie, I didn't know that *horses* liked you *too*."

With half an ear, as if she had heard the sounds from another world, Jenny was conscious of the fact that the band behind them had finally been able to play its fanfare. Obviously the program had begun, just as it had for more years than anyone could remember.

"Rascal," she said as she tightened the reins and turned toward Cecilia. "Rascal, I believe you're completely crazy."

Then, in an attempt to sound humorous and unconcerned, which almost came off, she added, "Listen, you don't know that girl. You're completely mistaken."

Cecilia laughed again, both at what Michael had said and at Rascal. She said nothing, but she took off her mitten, stretched out her hand, and petted Rascal, starting from the white "lantern" on her forehead and running her hand down to the horse's soft nose. Rascal raised her ears and nuzzled against Cecilia's red jacket again.

"She's tickling me," said Cecilia, almost bent double.

"I don't know what's gotten into her," Jenny said helplessly. "She doesn't usually behave like this."

From the castle steps the special Lucia Day song, the old Italian folk melody, "Santa Lucia," floated upwards. The words, which the crisp voices of the women sang out above the heads of the throng, had a tinge of Nordic melancholy in them.

"Land which the sun forgot,

Shadows sit down upon . . ."

The voices of the crowd were almost hushed. Near the castle wall Beauty and Pique remained as motionless as statues.

A dark-haired girl behind Cecilia whispered, "Isn't this the lovely horse you own yourself? You are probably Viveca Tornquist's sister, aren't you?"

Jenny nodded. It wasn't the first time she had heard herself identified in that fashion.

On the other hand, Cecilia, who had taken out a handkerchief and was trying to remove Rascal's slobberings, glanced at her hastily out of the corner of her eyes.

"You're Jenny, aren't you?" she asked. "Don't worry about this at all. She only wanted to show me that she liked me, didn't you, Rascal?"

"It's best if you stay right here now," said Michael to Jenny. "I have a feeling that we are just about to have some more music."

Applause broke out, first from the crowd standing immediately in front of the singers, then spreading like cracks in the ice, and finally thundering from all corners of the grounds. The festive mood had returned after being upset by all the confusion.

Lucia's countenance, small and heart-shaped under the weight of the crown of lights, was once again a smiling one and no longer pale. Jenny saw Viveca's lovely head of hair gleaming like a metal helmet in the light from the torches.

"Now I'll bet they're going to sing 'Steffan's Song,' " said Michael, who proved himself a true prophet even before he had come to the end of his sentence.

"Did you know or did you just take a guess?" Cecilia asked with a little giggle.

Jenny glanced warily at Cecilia. She suddenly began to feel that Rascal had been wise in choosing Cecilia Acker as the objective of her escapade that evening. Hereafter she would think of her in a different way. She puzzled a little over the feeling Cecilia aroused in her. It was pleasant, wistful, a little bit painful—the feeling you get when you raise your head on an April evening and become aware of opalescent, dizzying space . . .

"Oh, gosh! The riding instructor!" said Jenny suddenly. "What became of him?"

"If it's that tall character in the white fur coat you're referring to—the one that fell off—there's no need to worry about him," Michael said. "At the moment he is cavalierly helping your sister and the other attendants in through the gate. Look. You can see for yourself."

"That's terrible. I had almost forgotten about him," Jenny said ruefully. "Everything's my fault altogether. I was sitting there thinking about something else when Rascal all of a sudden got it into her head that she was going to come over here. No rider should ever let that happen."

These latter words were drowned in the music that the band, once again having assumed the leading role, had begun to play. The brass instruments glistened. The march, "Carl the King," echoed throughout the castle grounds.

Jenny bent forward in the saddle.

"Forgive us, Rascal and me," she said. With some effort she managed to catch Cecilia's eye. Jenny tried to think of something else to say, but nothing came out. She felt a little ashamed that she had lingered there a bit too long. With her heels she nudged Rascal and drew in one of the reins. Rascal began to move but none too willingly. As she rode slowly away, she was conscious that a number of eyes were watching her and her horse; it felt as if her neck were being hit by multitudes of darts.

But she wasn't at all aware of the serious interest that followed their smiles.

"Strange that she's Viveca Tornquist's sister," said Michael thoughtfully. "They aren't much alike, are they?"

Cecilia's gaze was still directed toward the straight little figure with her amusingly broad shoulders. Rascal's sweeping tail was so long that it almost touched the tops of the snowdrifts.

"You know," she said, "I think it's strange that Viveca Tornquist is *Jenny's* sister instead, if you understand what I mean." She laughed a little at the way she had expressed herself, but the others seemed in agreement.

At the foot of the castle steps, the riding instructor took great delight in telling Jenny what he thought of her.

"What the Sam Hill kind of horse do you think you're riding? An unmanageable jackass, perhaps? I'll tell you one thing, young lady. Neither you nor the horse is broken in. At least now I have an explanation for all the confusion up there. All we needed was someone like you, with no control over a horse, to exert your influence on all the riders and get everything fouled up."

Ingrid and Kristofer, on Pique and Beauty respectively, rode up on either side of Jenny, convinced that she needed moral support. Ingrid giggled at the riding instructor's final words, but Kristofer restricted himself to an encouraging wink. He had a great talent at expressing various feelings and points of view in this way.

Actually, the riding instructor was not half so furious as he seemed. He had found a whipping boy for the evening's failure, and in spite of the fact that the escapade with Rascal had been understood by only a few of the bystanders, he had become the object of much sympathy after his fall.

"I'm terribly sorry," Jenny mumbled. "I hope you didn't hurt yourself, sir."

"You have to be able to *fall*, too. That's a part of the training, my friend!"

Jenny's all-too-vivid mental picture of the riding instructor's flight through the air caused her to lower her head. Fortunately, he misinterpreted this gesture as an attempt, on Jenny's part, to hide the fact that she was about to burst into tears. His voice took on a fatherly quality as he continued.

"Well, anyway, it came out all right. I could give you some extra riding lessons when I have a little more time."

Ingrid glanced at Jenny out of the corner of her eye. With a strained voice, Kristofer managed to say, "How goes it with Palma, sir?"

"Oh, she's over there by the wing. They caught her almost immediately."

Jenny looked up and gave a sigh of relief. The crowd had thinned out sufficiently for the riders to begin to consolidate. Tarantella's rider was holding Palma's reins.

Suddenly the riding instructor gave a shrill blast on his by now familiar whistle.

"Assemble in formation for the ride back."

The standing torches had begun to flicker, smoke, and go out. Someone threw the one remaining torch into a snowdrift, where it died. Nevertheless, the castle courtyard was still almost as light as day. The moon had eased itself up over the castle gables and was casually casting its white light down upon the environs. In toward the castle wall was a more golden, warmer light, coming from the many high, lighted windows.

Like brooks beginning to run in the spring, the people of Nordvik hurried down the hill. Waves of voices and laughter sprang forth and died away between the park's huge, spreading linden trees. The sleighs, with their drivers and patient drays, began to look lonely and deserted as they waited down at the foot of the castle steps.

Pique and Rascal took their places at the head of the troops. Jenny was quiet and preoccupied. In her ears echoed the clear, concise question that Kristofer had formulated and posed just before they parted: "What ever gave Rascal the idea of searching for something in Cecilia's pocket?"

CHAPTER 11

A Gallop on the Ice

Behind drawn blinds the residents of Nordvik were asleep in their homes, which, in turn, slumbered behind a shroud of milk-white mist. Only those houses along the shore were distinguishable. Occasionally, in the faint light of the sunrise, their windows glistened like sleepy eyes that are reluctant to open and that quickly shut themselves and sink back into oblivion.

The first time they all rode on the ice on Nordvik Bay, Jenny amused herself by trying to pick out the familiar houses and parts of town, both of which seemed strange when viewed from a different perspective. But now, some weeks later, she was more fascinated instead by the perpetually shifting interplay of colors between the islands and out over the sea. You could almost imagine that the sun had risen as thoroughly rested and refreshed as Lars and Mona were in the morning and was playfully creating color spectacles in the sky and on the ice, which it wouldn't have strength for later in the day.

The horses were just as thoroughly rested and full of mischief. While still on the stable hill they had neighed to one another, and their eagerness to get down to the ice and their longing to gallop were unmistakable. Jenny her-

self was seized with mounting excitement and an almost
wild sense of expectation. A restless, shadowy memory suddenly surfaced: Wasn't this the way you often felt when you
were very little and the world was really new? When blue
was blue, and yellow was yellow, and red was breathlessly,
burningly red, more vivid than these colors would ever
again seem to your eyes, which had become all too familiar with everything? Like a swallow with pointed wings,
a thought pierced Jenny's mind: Is this maybe the real significance of growing up, of being mature, of growing old
—that nothing thereafter is ever really as white and glistening as the newly risen sun shining on the ice?

But the thought was merely a swallow, fleeting and
rapid, and it escaped even before Jenny had time to catch
it.

Still, the morning was new, just as the sun, just as the ice
—just as Rascal, who was only six years old.

There were eight riders under the supervision of their
own riding instructor, who was mounted on Beauty. They
had saddled their horses and nodded their greetings to one
another as they met that dark winter morning. But they
had deliberately refrained from talking in order not to risk
the loss of a single moment of the clean, pure contentment
that accompanied the expectation of a gallop on the ice.

Jenny gave the houses on the shore one parting glance,
in which there was a hint of wistfulness. In a way it would
have been wonderful, as she knew very well, to sleep
dreamlessly and late during the Christmas vacation, beyond those first greedy hours of the morning. But this desire was nothing that really needed to be surmounted as

long as Rascal and the ice were waiting for her. The mist was disappearing now with the coming of the wind off the land, and the sunbeams on the snow crystals were as playful as kittens.

Starting from the brush and bushes on the shore at Ekenase Wall, they rode down onto the ice. From years of experience, the riding instructor knew every inlet and bay, every current, and the meaning behind every shift of the ice. While they were still at a walking pace, he would share this knowledge with those who rode close to him. As yet, they still had time and attention to spare for their surroundings.

Between the islands a wide channel had been broken through the ice. The sunbeams, having just discovered the barriers that had been put up, were playfully dancing among the blocks of ice. Straight through the channel, a powerful black cargo steamer, flying a foreign flag, was moving with great dignity. Slowly and smoothly it progressed like a boat being towed across a theater stage. Both the immovable floor of ice, which stretched out before them, and the eerie, reflected light caused the ship to seem artificial and the whole scene more than a shade unreal.

Still at a walking pace, the riders hugged the shore. Jenny was forced to hold the reins on Rascal because the horse's eagerness was just about to spill over the brim. There was a small bay and one more promontory, and after that came the community's last outpost with the shipyard and the long piers. Now the ice lay ahead as far as the eye could see. Powdered with light snow, strong, and safe, it seemed to (and, in actual fact, did) go all the way to

Lindeby, a neighboring town. The woods were dense along the shore, and the greenness stood out sharply against the world of white that prevailed in the light of dawn.

Here the waters of the bay were blue in the spring; here in June came the pike and the perch; here . . .

"Keep ten yards' distance between your horses," shouted the riding instructor. "Farther away, Peter. Everybody ready? Gallop!"

Actually, it was just those few seconds before and the moments immediately after the gallop on the ice when Jenny felt her greatest thrill. In the midst of the gallop she neither felt nor thought about anything. Everything, which under other circumstances was real and meaningful —such as her grades, Christmas presents, the dances she would be invited to during the vacation—disappeared like mud sinking to the bottom of a river bed.

Sometimes the ice would strain and crackle under the riders. She remembered how it had frightened her the first time, but later on, when she knew this meant only that the ice was frozen way down deep, the sound became exciting and fell into place as just a small part of the total experience.

As a shield against the wind, Jenny had on her long, bright blue jacket with its leather-trimmed hood, which she pulled up over her crash helmet and which also covered her cheeks and her chin. It was a curious thing. Right after the gallop she could be soaked with perspiration, but, nevertheless, during the ride certain parts of her body, especially her hands and chin, could simultaneously become chilled so thoroughly as to have lost all feeling.

These were the things that brought her back down to earth afterwards.

Also in this category belonged the thrill of telling her astonished family that she had been in Lindeby with Rascal that morning. The distance between the two towns was quite great if you were to travel by car, but the journey over the frozen bays took less than half an hour. Even Lars eyed her respectfully at the breakfast table.

The streets in Lindeby were interesting and unfamiliar. The group slowed down to a walk, and the horses were relaxed and calm after their vigorous exercise. The feeling of utter freedom, light, pure as the snow at the Lindeby shore, was still with the riders. The gallop home over the ice was still to come.

Jenny was conscious of the smooth, rhythmic beat of hoofs on either side, in front of, and behind her.

"You don't need to say a word to anybody here," Jenny thought. "It's nice just to have friends . . ."

"Just to have friends around you . . ." Rascal seemed to take up the thought and moved a little closer to Beauty.

As they approached Nordvik Bay and walked slowly home over the familiar stretch of ice, a feeling of fatigue, brought on by tremendous exertion, welled up and engulfed Jenny. Under the jacket hood her hair stuck to her temples, but she had to move her fingers vigorously, one after the other to get the circulation into them again. Out there in the high, clear air the breath from the horses' nostrils appeared in the shape of strange mushrooms.

While they had been away, Nordvik had awakened. They met a few skaters while they were still far out on the ice.

Here and there could be seen a sailboat on the way toward the small islands. Farther in toward land they saw skiers and pedestrians. Right at the shore the ice had been cleaned off as a skating rink, and there the isolated signs of life gave way to colorful, noisy groups. It was Christmas vacation, of course.

Just as they passed the skating rink, they met Kristofer. Jenny had recognized him from far away because he had Ramrod with him. For a change, Ramrod was on a leash because he regarded as fair game anything and everything that moved around swiftly, and the motion of the skaters constituted irresistible temptation. Jenny was so hot and breathless after a gallop that she saw everything around her more or less through a pink fog, which obliterated faces and details. She was vaguely aware that a group of boys and girls was following Kristofer, but she paid no particular attention to them, although they came quite close.

But Rascal paid attention to them. Quite unexpectedly, the horse came to such a dead stop that Jenny nearly flew over her head. Ingrid, who was behind them on Pique, managed, only by a quick maneuver to the right, to escape bumping Rascal from the rear.

There was no feeling of panic—just dumfounded amazement. They had been going along at a walking pace, and Jenny was too relaxed to panic. But for a brief second she began to wonder if she had fallen asleep on the back of the horse. Or had she just been sitting there dreaming?

Right before her eyes appeared a red jacket with a familiar zipper pocket, and Cecilia Acker's no less familiar blue eyes, this time agape with unadulterated, undeniable astonishment.

"Now *this* is going too far," Jenny said with real conviction. She turned her head and watched helplessly as her comrades disappeared. Ingrid waved at her.

Cecilia's eyes were almost shut as she dissolved in a fit of laughter. Energetically, Rascal nuzzled against the closed pocket, and a tumult of voices broke out.

"There's that same horse again."

"Do you usually go around with sugar in your pocket, Cecilia?"

"He's in love with her, can't you see? He can't let her alone."

"Silly, that's no he; it's a she."

While the others were catching their breath, Kristofer intervened. He seemed to have been waiting all his life for just that one moment.

"This is extremely interesting," he said emphatically. "We are being treated to a very valuable glimpse into this horse's psyche and reactions. It seems to me, at least, that we have previously only scratched the surface."

Strangely enough, the others listened in silence. Ramrod turned his back to Rascal and looked longingly out over the ice. He continued to think the horse was just too big.

"Cecilia," Kristofer continued. "Had you ever met Rascal before the Lucia parade?"

"Never," Cecilia said positively.

"And you don't go sneaking up to her stall to give her sugar on the sly?"

"Are you crazy? I'm scared to death of horses."

A peal of laughter greeted her answer, which had been given, obviously, from the depths of her heart.

Rascal launched a new attack on the jacket pocket. Meaningfully she smacked her lips. The innocent by-standers looked at each other in utter bewilderment.

"We'll have to concentrate on her subconscious," Kristofer said. "Smell. I think I've got it; just wait and see. How about it? Are you scented in some special way, Cecie? Michael, you must know something about that."

"Oh, stop it!" Cecilia pleaded, blushing frantically. Her complexion was so transparent that she couldn't hide her feelings.

"Roses and lilies," Michael declared. Declining to look at anyone, he studiously gazed at the ice.

"I'm awfully sorry," Jenny said as she looked up toward the shore. "There are the others up there waiting for me. I'm afraid I've got to run along. You can let me know later if you reach any decision, Kristofer. It's all beyond me, I must say. But so long."

"So long," they cried after her.

Jenny and Rascal trotted. The other riders were already on the road, and Jenny decided to use one of the short cuts diagonally across the shore. She had ridden Rascal there previously, but, just to be on the safe side, she slowed her down to a walk. Rascal took purposeful steps, but although she continued along the way without hesitation, Jenny could sense that Rascal was disappointed that she hadn't found what she wanted with Cecilia. She was looking for something good to eat . . . but why just with Cecilia? It was completely ununderstandable; Jenny shook her head.

They were up among the thorny bushes now where the snow barely covered the ground. Suddenly a stone rolled into their path, and Rascal stumbled.

"Oooh," Jenny cried. "Rascal, you poor thing. Did you hurt yourself?"

For the next few seconds Rascal's steps seemed somewhat hesitant, so much so that Jenny considered getting off to look at her hoofs. But presently they caught up with the waiting riders, and Jenny had no desire to delay them any longer, especially since Rascal seemed to be walking completely normally on the smooth, snow-covered road.

"I'm so sorry," Jenny said as she rode up to join the riding instructor. "It was Rascal who stopped. I don't know what's gotten into her. That's the second time she has acted peculiarly."

The riding instructor gave a small laugh.

"She probably recognized someone," he suggested, "and hoped for an extra allowance. That girl with the bright red jacket, for example. I remember a mare once who was crazy about red simply because I had a red scarf, and it was always I who used to feed her."

"But I don't even own anything red except a party dress, and Rascal has certainly never seen that," Jenny remarked helplessly.

"Perhaps she has other friends who have something red," replied the riding instructor.

Jenny fell into silence. This had never occurred to her, but it opened up possibilities. What if someone really were riding Rascal in secret—someone who had an article of clothing that was bright red? Of course you could eliminate

Cecilia right off. Her fear of horses and her genuine astonishment were certainly not put on, and, except for Kristofer, Jenny had never seen either her or any of her friends at the Riding Academy.

They chose quiet streets for their ride through Nordvik. A few isolated tire tracks had made patterns in the snow, but otherwise the snow on the streets and sidewalks lay flat, like newly ironed sheets.

On the hedges and the old, knotted branches of the fruit trees the snow had settled in the shape of soft pillows, and a couple of gables on the old houses looked as if they were wearing nightcaps. The buildings seemed to stretch themselves and awaken, bathed in the bright yellow sunshine. Jenny's thoughts lingered over the new idea that the riding instructor's words had given her. It was more or less the same idea that Kristofer had attempted to express when he asked about smells. Could it be that the appearance—and not the smell—was the factor?

Later as they rode over the railroad tracks and started up the hill toward the stables, Jenny found something else to puzzle over. The first thing that commanded her attention was that Rascal made a curious movement with her head. It was just as if she had dropped off to sleep momentarily. Almost simultaneously Jenny noticed that they were lagging behind Beauty, who was now leading them by a couple of lengths. This was surprising; usually, with the stalls and the cribs so enticingly near, the horses were in a great hurry. Cautiously and with some hesitation Rascal took the last steps leading up to the stables. Jenny, now extra alert, felt that Rascal wasn't placing her right forefoot down on the ground as hard as she did the others. Was it possible that she had sprained something when they took that short cut a while back?

After dismounting in the stable yard Jenny calmly stroked Rascal's nose and neck. The horse stood with her head lowered, not once glancing expectantly at the stall door as she usually did. Jenny bent down and examined her right foreleg but found nothing unusual. She didn't dare to trust her own limited judgment, but went instead and got the riding instructor after she had taken Rascal into her stall.

"She stumbled on a loose rock when we were riding up from the ice," Jenny explained. "And now during this whole last stretch I thought she seemed so unlike herself. It was just as if she were afraid to put her right forefoot down. But I can't find anything wrong myself."

The riding instructor gently moved his hand along from the knee down to the right hoof. He repeated this gesture with the left forefoot.

"There's no swelling," he said. He put his hand on the right fetlock, then on the left, and, once again, on the right. He gave a slight whistle.

"Feel right here, Jenny," he said. "The right one is much warmer—quite hot, in fact. Don't you think so?"

Jenny nodded. She looked so frightened that the riding instructor began to comfort her.

"It's nothing dangerous, but it was really fortunate that you discovered it this early. It's probably a slight sprain, but if you were to ride her any more, she might begin to be lame, and then the whole thing would be very difficult to take care of."

Once more Jenny felt along Rascal's right fetlock.

"Now I'm sure I can feel a little swelling here on the side."

"There could be a little, of course, but there's no denying that it feels warm. If you'll just let her rest a couple of days, I think it will clear up all by itself. This is just why it's so good that you know your horse as well as you do."

Jenny went to get an extra ration of oats for Rascal, and then she groomed her and cleaned her hoofs carefully. Rascal pricked up her ears and seemed completely herself again. Ingrid came and offered some sugar to Rascal, and some chewing gum, as well as her heartfelt sympathy, to Jenny.

Gunilla promised to take special care of Rascal during the afternoon and evening.

"And how about Bengt?" Jenny asked. "Will you tell him about this when he comes, Gunilla?"

"He's not coming any more today," Gunilla replied, with a small giggle. "He has the day off. He came in while all of you were out riding, and you should have seen how elegant he was in his bright red jacket and new riding breeches. I think he was impressed by that substitute riding instructor and his red riding habit, and now he wants to be just as elegant himself."

"No, that has nothing to do with it," Ingrid assured her. "He has had that jacket a long time, although he uses it only when he rides, and lately he hasn't been riding too often. He has a lot to do; the stables are bursting with horses."

"I guess you're right," said Gunilla. "But I haven't time to stand here talking."

She went off to help a beginner who was not yet skilled in the art of saddling and who had cried out for help.

"She's very nice," Jenny said absently. "Listen, don't you think that it's mostly girls who have red jackets? How does Bengt look in his?"

Ingrid thought the question was trifling and she answered it accordingly.

"Oh," she said, "it's so seldom that he has it on—only when he's riding, as I said before, and when it's cold. Are you going home now? Can we go together?"

Jenny nodded. Ingrid thought her friend seemed pre-occupied. She had no way of knowing, of course, that all the way home they were accompanied by an invisible companion, a figure with indistinct features but dressed in a very clear bright coat—a red jacket with a zipper pocket.

CHAPTER 12

Decision and Action

Jenny, deep in thought, escorted the invisible, red-jacketed companion home and up to her room. She locked the door after her and pretended not to hear Mona's sorrowful appeal for Jenny to read her a story.

"We can take one about horses, Jenny," she pleaded, but to no avail.

A little while later, though, it was impossible to turn a deaf ear. Lars, who had a cold and was confined to the house, began to play ice hockey in the hall right outside her door. Sheer might and power often conquer, but in this case it was sheer noise that triumphed.

Jenny gave up all hope of collecting her thoughts and opened the door.

"Why are you sitting in there looking so sour?" Lars asked immediately as he alertly observed his sister.

Somewhat bitterly, Jenny decided that it didn't pay to have an even, happy disposition. Viveca could mope around, silent and ill-humored for days on end, with no one in the family paying the slightest attention. On the contrary, voices were lowered, and appropriate discretion was observed. But if she, Jenny, behaved similarly, even for a few hours, no one failed to comment.

Now Mona had joined them. "Are you worried about something, Jenny? Tell me."

Then from the lower regions of the house came her mother's voice.

"Jenny, why haven't you eaten your breakfast? Don't you feel well? I get so worried about your galloping on the ice in this cold weather."

Jenny choked down her vexation. But she was fair-minded by nature, and she had to admit to herself that she couldn't very well beg for sympathy if she didn't let her family in on her troubles.

"I'll be down in just a minute to eat a sandwich, Mother. And you don't need to worry one bit—it was simply wonderful on the ice." Then to Mona she said, "If you can find a nice story about horses or some other animal, I'll read to you a little while as soon as I've eaten."

Mona disappeared, buzzing like a contented bee who has found its heart's desire among the flowers.

Jenny followed a different course of action with Lars. He needed to be handled more objectively.

"I am a little worried, you see, because Rascal got some kind of sprain when we were riding this morning. Nothing dangerous, but she'll have to stay in the stall for a couple of days."

"Hmmm," said Lars reflectively, as he hit the hockey puck. It landed in its "cage" under the sewing machine.

Jenny found sandwiches, eggs, and a Thermos with hot chocolate on the kitchen table. She had forgotten how hungry she was, and she discovered, to her delight, that food seemed to stimulate her thought process. In addition, amazingly enough, she was allowed to satisfy her appetite in absolute peace. She leaned back against the deliciously warm radiator, able to think at last.

Was it really within the realm of possibility that some stranger was taking Rascal out and riding her in secret? Jenny's thoughts moved back over these last weeks, and she mused over what had happened. A saddle hung up backwards—sand and clay stuck in Rascal's hoof. Both of these things could perhaps be explained away pretty easily. But Jenny knew that it wasn't these obvious things that were speaking to her so plainly. No. It was the change that had come over Rascal. Vague things. Diffuse things. But all very plain and unmistakable to Jenny. She had to admit, without reservation, that there was nothing that should really make her worry. Rascal was not any the worse off, didn't seem afraid, certainly hadn't been badly treated. Somewhere, perhaps in a detective story, Jenny had recently seen the expression, "an outside influence." She was certain, both by reason and by instinct, that Rascal had come under some "outside influence."

Slowly she chewed her food and took a deep gulp from her chocolate mug. She didn't want to run the risk of losing her train of thought.

The red jacket—could that be the answer to the riddle? Perhaps. In any case, there weren't very many possible solutions to the mystery, and she had to exploit what little there was. Here, at least, was a starting point.

She had reached one of the milestones. Whom could she suspect? Well, who could get into the stalls during the early morning hours? There were two keys. One was always in the possession of the riding instructor. The other was shared by Gunilla and Bengt. They always put it in a crack between the stones on the gable that faced down toward the enclosure. Since Jenny was often the first one in the stalls in the morning, she had been told where the key was kept. It was an excellent hiding place; the key was completely concealed, and the gable was pretty high up. No stranger was apt to come upon it by accident, and, as far as Jenny knew, she was the only one, except for the riding instructor and the two employees of the stable, who knew of its whereabouts.

Back to Bengt. Jenny sat poised, with the chocolate mug halfway to her mouth. She thought about Bengt for quite a while—body and soul. His tall, gangly body, his jerky movements, which, nevertheless, were so coordinated and controlled whenever he had anything to do with the animals, his coarse manners. She knew that Bengt hadn't seemed very friendly to her lately. He had almost come right out and said that he didn't think Jenny deserved to own a horse such as Rascal. It's always difficult to admit that someone else doesn't like you. Jenny had charged his feeling off to jealousy.

She had heard all the gossip about Bengt's past. People had hinted at a "suspended sentence" and "probationary supervision." The stable was not a place where there was much gossip, because everyone there was occupied with more important things, but the rumors were, nonetheless, over town. Since Bengt *had* been friendly to all the riders and had performed his duties beyond reproach, the rumors seemed to have heightened his popularity, not lessened it.

Jenny remembered how nice and helpful he had been with Lars. As she sat thinking about him, she discovered that she couldn't really bring herself to dislike him. But there *was* Ingrid's tidbit about his red jacket . . .

Whom else could she suspect? Gunilla? Gunilla who was so sleepy in the mornings that she could scarcely keep her eyes open the first hour or so at the stables? Gunilla—conscientious, reliable, not overly bright? Jenny had to laugh at the idea. It was so absurd as to be out of the question.

Was it imaginable that someone—an outsider—had kept watch one morning and seen where Jenny got the key? Or where Gunilla or Bengt had come to get it? When it came right down to it, it would not have been very difficult for any interested party to make it his business to find out where the hiding place was.

Jenny's thoughts came rushing. She put her chocolate mug down on the table. Almost unconsciously she poked among the bread crumbs with her fingertips. Her hands suddenly felt icy.

This mysterious person—if such there were, and if he or she were an outsider—would have no way of knowing about the sprain Rascal had gotten. Jenny had purposely been careful to ask Gunilla to tell Bengt—but if the borrower of the horse were someone else . . . ? If this person decided to ride Rascal tomorrow morning, even with her bad leg . . . ?

Jenny's movements were suddenly no longer meaningless. She got up so quickly that the stool on which she had been sitting fell back and struck the radiator.

Jenny had never shared Lars's passion for detective

stories or adventures. Now she surprised herself at her ability to think and do things just as brave and daring, to break away from her everyday pattern just as positively as any heroine in a book. She knew the reason. She had sensed the danger that threatened Rascal.

She would keep watch over the horse herself. She would expose and get rid of the "outside influence."

Within a few seconds Jenny had examined the possibilities, thought about her difficulties, and conquered them. This evening she would sneak out without anyone's knowing it. Even if her suspicions proved to be groundless, no one could laugh at her afterwards. It would be a simple thing for her to hide somewhere in the stalls or in the hayloft; Gunilla need not notice a thing, even if she were the last one to leave the stalls. It was nice and warm at the academy, and there were lots and lots of blankets. Jenny wouldn't need to freeze. The stable door would have to remain locked, and the key would have to stay in its usual hiding place, so that the secret rider would find it, as usual, and not begin to suspect something.

Jenny decided to pretend to go to bed early here at home —something that would meet with her parents' undivided approval. In the morning no one would miss her. Most mornings, of course, she was the first one up and out of the house. She could manage to rumple up her bed convincingly enough.

"Jenny!" A voice of complaint rose from the nursery. "Aren't you *ever* coming?"

"I'll be there in a minute, Mona. Wait just a little bit longer."

Jenny made rapid progress. She put a pot of water on the hot plate. She climbed up onto the sink. From there she could get down a little Thermos bottle, which, now that the family was bigger, was seldom or never used. No one would ever miss it.

While the tea water boiled, Jenny made a little pile of sandwiches. Bread and butter and cheese were easy to come by. But it was important that she get everything done before someone came out into the kitchen and discovered what she was up to. Just as the first bubbles appeared on the surface of the water, she put the sandwiches she had made and a couple of tea bags in a little plastic box. She knew she might have a long night of it, and she didn't want to fall asleep during her vigil.

She rinsed out the Thermos bottle, filled it with hot water, and corked it. In the pantry she found a sack of apples and put one in her little stock of provisions.

While she stood there a couple of seconds longer, considering what else she could take that no one would miss, she suddenly heard a noise over by the door.

Jenny had thought she was being very calm and cool in her actions. But when the unexpected noise alerted her, she discovered that she had been in a state of great excitement the whole time. Her heart leaped up into her throat; quick as lightning she turned around. Her sack of food lay behind her on the counter.

There in the doorway stood Lars. He had on his turtleneck wool sweater, and his hands were stuffed in his pants pockets. Apparently deep in thought, he shifted from one

foot to the other and searchingly examined the devastated breakfast table.

"It's fantastic what you managed to stuff into yourself," he commented. "French bread, brown bread, half the rye bread, and all of the butter!"

"So what?" Jenny sputtered. Her heart was no longer in her throat, but it was still beating frantically. She was very well aware of both her own inability to fib without being self-conscious and Lars's uncanny talent for seeing through her fibs. "What business is this of yours?"

Lars took a long, speculative look around the kitchen.

"Oh, you learn this and that when you study about detectives," he remarked with complete indifference.

Jenny attempted to look unconcerned and to behave as if nothing had happened; at the same time she tried, unobtrusively, to keep the sack of food hidden behind her as long as possible.

"It's a shame that a person can't even get enough to eat around this house without some comment from you," she said boldly.

At that moment, just as Lars was about to turn his attention from the breakfast table to the sack of food, there was a welcome interruption.

Viveca appeared on the scene.

"Listen, you two!" she said, placing herself right in the middle of the kitchen with her hands on her hips. "I want to tell you something, and I want you to listen, both of you. You especially, Lars."

Lars, momentarily jolted from his position as "official watchman," grew very sober. He forgot both Jenny and his suspicions. Viveca wouldn't let him look away for a minute.

"Gustav is coming here with me this evening," she said, "to help me with a physics experiment. We thought we would like to sit here in the kitchen and have some tea, so after seven o'clock I don't want a whole stream of people going back and forth through the room. Especially a parade of seven-year-old characters who come down to filch apples from the pantry. Do I make myself clear?"

While Viveca raved and ranted, Jenny regained her self-possession. She realized that the least suspicious thing would be to go about her business and act as if nothing had happened. With no attempt to conceal what she was doing, she took the sack of sandwiches and the Thermos, opened a cupboard, and put them on a shelf. In front of them she placed a couple of small sacks of flour, and then she shut the door.

"Mona, I'm coming now," she said loudly.

Her strategy was working better than she could have expected. No one paid any attention to her. She was calm and in control of herself. Behind her she could hear Viveca and Lars exchanging the usual acid comments.

"You and your old stupid boy friends."

"Why don't you ever tie your shoes? Do you think it's *illegal* to look nice?"

"No, but I have begun to wonder since I saw you in that new thing you just bought. Do you call that a dress?"

Immediately thereafter, steps flew up the stairs. Lars had made his retreat.

CHAPTER 13

Jenny Goes into Action

During the afternoon, Jenny managed, at a moment when no one was watching, to sneak into the kitchen, gather up her provisions, and hide them in her own closet. She was very pleased with the way things were going. To be sure, she had heard her mother muttering something about the marvelous appetite Jenny had had after her ride on the ice, but Mother's voice had sounded more pleased than surprised. Lars seemed to have forgotten his suspicions of the morning and was completely lost in his ice-hockey practice. In the main, Lars lived in a world of fantasy, seldom close to reality, and any casual listener would have gotten the impression that at least half the Swedish International Hockey Team had gathered in the upstairs hall in the Tornquist home.

"Foul. Made by Mats Blomblad. Gunvar out. Tumba in. Bantam goes to the attack. Opposition at the Russian goal; the goal watcher tries in vain. Go-o-o-o-o-al!"

These shouts were accompanied by an inordinate number of slides across the floor and tremendous crashes of small feet against the woodwork. Jenny, who was trying to lay the plans for the evening, longed desperately for the day when Lars would be over his cold and could once again get rid of his excess energy out on the skating rink.

She found that everything was playing right into her hands. Her mother and father planned to be away that evening, and Viveca was to be responsible for seeing that Mona was in bed by seven o'clock. In addition, that business of Gustav's being in the kitchen opened up hitherto unthought of possibilities. If everything went according to her calculations, Jenny would not need to climb down from her window and make her way over the garage roof, as she had at first planned, not without some misgivings. The biggest problem was that Lars, who couldn't be forced into bed before nine o'clock during the Christmas vacation, was stretched out flat in front of the television set in the hall, where he could at the same time keep an alert eye peeled toward the main door. Jenny had to be in the stall at eight o'clock, at the latest. Somewhere around eight-thirty, Gunilla generally gave the horses their water and made a final inspection before she locked up for the night.

Consequently, it was of the utmost importance that Jenny get out without letting Lars see her.

About seven-thirty she joined him and watched television. She noticed, to her great satisfaction, that he was completely carried away by the program—a documentary about the jungles of India. When Jenny yawned, as she had carefully planned to do, and announced, "I'm going to bed now. I've been up since six o'clock this morning," the only response was an impatient grunt from the small figure in front of the television.

From the bottom of the stairway Jenny shouted her

parting words. "Please try to be quiet when you go up to bed later on. Don't stick your nose into my room because I plan to go right to sleep. If you do, you'll *never* get to ride Rascal."

If Lars gave her any answer, it was drowned in a roar emanating from a hungry leopard. Jenny disappeared up the stairs. She was pleased with herself at having been so natural about the whole thing. Lars had also behaved just as she had figured he would—he did nothing at all.

Once in her room, Jenny worked quickly and methodically. Out came her clothes—the heaviest she owned. Earlier she had smuggled her jacket up from the downstairs closet. The bed had already been rumpled up so that it would look as if she had slept in it, in the event that someone should happen to come in in the morning. Into a big bag went her sack of food. Heavy mittens, sugar lumps, and hard bread for Rascal . . .

Jenny turned out her light. Cautiously, noiselessly, she opened her door. She listened. Were there any sounds in the house? On the upstairs floor it was so quiet that she could hear Mona's even breathing through the half-open door to the nursery. From down below she could hear the faint, indefinite sounds coming from the jungles of India.

It remained to be seen if Viveca would react in accordance with Jenny's expectations. She giggled softly to herself, and while still on the stairs going down to the kitchen, she took a deep breath and tried to assume as carefree an air as possible. Happily humming to herself, she opened the door and entered the kitchen.

Gustav and Viveca sat on opposite sides of the kitchen

table. The appealing smell of newly toasted bread was everywhere.

"Well! What do you know?" said Jenny in mock surprise. "Are *you* here?"

Viveca gave her a chilling look. Gustav looked up in a much more friendly manner. He even nodded. Jenny looked at him amiably.

"Oh, don't let me disturb you!" she continued exuberantly. "I'm just going down to the library with a couple of books. Good-by now." She took a couple of long-drawn-out steps over toward the outside door. Now—now, surely Viveca would make some remark. Jenny laid her hand on the doorknob.

A spoon rattled as it fell on a china plate.

"I just want to say one thing," said Viveca in a menacingly subdued voice. "Please come in the front door when you come back. The floor here has just been scrubbed."

This was even better than Jenny could have dreamed up herself. She gave Gustav such a nice smile that he actually looked surprised.

"Yes, sure. I will," she said happily. "You'll lock up carefully when Gustav goes, won't you, Viveca? I'm going right up to bed when I come home. So long."

Things had progressed beyond her wildest expectations. Laughing merrily to herself, Jenny hid her face in the hood of her jacket as she ran down the road. She glanced hastily at her watch. It wasn't even eight o'clock yet. She slowed down and tried to catch her breath. She could take it easy and think out just how she was going to manage everything.

The roads lay quiet and deserted. Not a person was in sight. High above Nordvik arched the dark and cloudy sky, but toward the north there was, as always, a light, faintly reddish glow, the reflection from the multitudes of lights in the neighboring big city.

The air was bitingly cold, but Jenny felt warm and happy. And she wasn't afraid of the bleakness, of being alone. She had always considered that being alone was being in company with yourself. Every corner and turn of the road was familiar to her, and from the hills and the valleys the lights from familiar, friendly windows blinked. A pheasant, who for some reason hadn't found shelter for the night, had taken roost on a gatepost. He sat there with regal dignity and with bold tail feathers standing straight up. As Jenny came into view, he took fright, lost his dignity, and presently surprised a whole harem of hens in an adjacent hedge. Wings flapped; snow flew; strange, hoarse cries filled the air.

Jenny crossed the railroad tracks. At first she had the sinking feeling that all was quiet and dark at the riding academy up there on the hill. Her heart pounded wildly. What if Gunilla had finished her work and had gone away earlier than usual? However, she finally saw a gleam of light through the trees. It shone from the high, narrow window of the office, which faced out toward the gable. Everything was just as it should be. She was positive that Gunilla was still sitting there working on the account books.

Purposely Jenny let her steps lag. There was no hurry. There, not very far away, were warmth and comfort. There were the stables in which she felt so at home. She decided she would prolong the expectant moments as she wandered up the hill.

Now what? Were the pheasants crazy tonight? Or . . . what was moving there in the hedges over near the barn?

No! It certainly was something much bigger than a pheasant. A dog, perhaps. Or even a person. The path that led up to the stables was badly lighted, even for Nordvik. Jenny unconsciously moved a little faster as she went by the suspicious bushes.

"BOO!"

Jenny jumped quickly to one side. After she found out what it was that had frightened her, she breathed a big sigh of relief. Pooh. It was only a little boy! But then . . .

"Lars, what in heaven's name are you doing here?"

"Ha, ha, ha, ha, ha!"

Her scare, the subsequent relief, the new fright as she began to grasp the real meaning of Lars's appearance on the scene—everything exploded within Jenny all at once. The sparks began to fly; combustion set in. Jenny stamped her foot on the ground.

"Don't just stand there grinning! What are you doing here?" she asked angrily.

Lars, who radiated triumph from the blunt toes of his Lapland boots to the pompom on his knitted cap, subsided. He recognized the wrath in Jenny's voice. Very seldom was this sort of mood prevalent in their family.

"I was just following you, Jenny!"

"You know very well that you aren't supposed to be out at this time of night. You make me sick. You're terrible, Lars!"

Vigorously Jenny stamped her foot again. Lars hung his head.

"Nobody knows about it, Jenny. I sneaked away just like you did. And I have my own sack of food, so you don't need to worry that you're going to have to give me any of yours."

Slowly but surely the dawn came to Jenny. The full significance of Lars's words hit her. She glanced fretfully up in the direction of the stable buildings. There was still a light in the office.

"How did you know that I was going to come here?"

"I saw everything—when you made sandwiches, and fixed tea, and when you hid all your stuff. It was perfectly obvious that you were going to come and sleep here in Rascal's stall because she is sick and all that. And you yawned so much and were so dramatic before you went to bed. Usually you never say a word when you go up to bed in the evenings. But what you said made me positive. I'm a detective, you know."

Lars had finished talking. His self-consciousness began to return, and he tried to hide his head in his jacket.

Jenny had also had time to come to her senses. Now she spoke to him calmly and in control, but sarcastically.

"Very interesting, all of it. And now you march straight home and go to bed and keep quiet about this. Not so much as a word, you understand! Otherwise, you'll never even get to come near Rascal as long as you live!"

Lars stood with his legs far apart. He had been prepared for this. He began to dig his heels into the snow as if he were trying to hold his own against the superior forces of nature.

"No."

"What do you mean 'no' if I may ask?"

"No, I'm not going home. I think I'll stay and sleep with Rascal too."

"Don't make me laugh! Go on home now."

There was dead silence for a couple of seconds. It was obvious that, on Lars's part, the pause was strategic. As he spoke, his words came out slowly, and each syllable was accented.

"O.K. I'll go home. And ring the bell at the front door. And Viveca will come and open it. What do you think she will say? 'Lars, where in the world did you come from?' And I will answer, 'I was with Jenny. At the stables. She's going to stay there all night.' "

There, under the dark, gnarled linden trees, the silence hung heavily. Below in the valley a lonely train went swiftly along like a huge lightning bug. Lars pretended to be following it with his glance, but out of the corners of his eyes he was observing Jenny intently.

Her whole body grew hot. Would her well-laid plans for the vigil with Rascal be ruined completely just because of her unbearable little brother? And Rascal! If someone were to ride her, it could mean that the slight sprain might turn into something worse. Jenny was aware of how serious such injuries could be. Rascal might be lamed.

Jenny looked inquiringly at Lars. She saw his red cheeks, his eyes, which were almost popping out of his head with eagerness and excitement, and she noticed, too, that they were somber and defiant.

Time was slipping by. Even if she could succeed somehow in talking some sense into him, she wouldn't have the time. And then, too, the night and the vigil that lay before her were going to be long and lonely. Jenny knew from experience that if you treated Lars as your equal and as a friend, he could be wonderful—loyal, trustworthy, and patient. Jenny made her decision.

"Are you absolutely 100 per cent certain that no one saw you when you left the house?"

"I swear. Viveca thinks that I went to bed."

"But when Mother and Dad come home, they'll surely look in to see if you are asleep!"

"They'll just look from the doorway. They don't dare go clear up to the bed because they're always afraid of waking me. I'm very easily awakened, you know. And before I left, I put some cushions under the covers. And I messed up the covers, and I put Mona's doll on my pillow. From the doorway it will look just as if I am in there snoring away."

What Lars said was true. No one would actually dare to come up close to his bed. For that matter, it was too late to do anything about it now. She couldn't take the risk.

"Okay. Come with me. But you'll have to listen and do just *exactly* as I say."

"I will. Oh, Jenny, I really will. Just exactly as you say, Jenny."

"Listen carefully now. Stand there in the bushes where you hid before. After a while, about fifteen minutes or maybe longer, I can't say just how long, Gunilla will be coming by here. Sit still and be quiet as a mouse until she has disappeared. Then sneak up to the stable door and I'll let you in."

Jenny considered this to be the safest course of action.

It might be awkward to have Lars in there with her from the beginning.

Lars had been transformed into a receiving station. He shook his head up and down to show her that he understood.

"Get going," said Jenny curtly.

Lars disappeared into the bushes like a rabbit going down into his hole. There was no doubt that he understood the art of sitting motionless, because when Jenny crossed the yard, there wasn't a sound or motion anywhere.

Just as Jenny had expected, Gunilla was alone in the stables. She had come down from the office and was busy filling the cribs and the water troughs.

"Well, what brings you here this time of night?"

"I just wanted to look at Rascal one more time. Have you examined her leg?"

"Yes, and I don't think there's anything. But I've noticed that she doesn't like to put any weight on it."

Jenny was already in the stall with Rascal, who was greatly excited over this late and unexpected visit. She shook her ears and nuzzled Jenny's side mischievously.

While Jenny stood bent over the horse's leg and felt carefully with her fingers along the feverish fetlock, she heard the click of Gunilla's wooden shoes as she made her way toward the stable entrance. With caution, Jenny stuck her head out from the stall.

Gunilla disappeared into the farthest stall where Hoppsan was. Hoppsan was a favorite. Gunilla would probably be in there for a few minutes.

Quickly Jenny moved along between the rows of horses over toward the other side of the stable where the office and the arena were. The office door was locked, but the key was still in the lock. The door to the arena opened at Jenny's cautious shove. It creaked, and Jenny's brain was dizzy as she searched for a plausible explanation in the event that Gunilla had heard anything. "I was just going to see if you had turned off the lights in there . . . I thought I saw a light down on the road . . . I was just going to see if I had left a newspaper up in the loft . . . I was just . . ."

But Gunilla didn't notice anything. Jenny left the door to the arena ajar and, like a shadow, crept quickly back to Rascal.

"The joint isn't swollen at all, I guess," she said happily when Gunilla came back along the passage.

Gunilla mumbled something inaudible. She was tired after her long day's work and didn't especially welcome a visitor at closing time. Still she sympathized with Jenny. If you owned a horse as wonderful as Rascal . . . and Jenny was never arrogant, nor did she come up with a lot of unreasonable requests as did some of the grownups who owned horses in the stables.

Wearily, but with no unfriendliness, Gunilla said, "I'm going to lock up now, and I really prefer to do it myself. Just for the sake of order."

"I'll run along in a minute. I'm just going to have a few more minutes with Rascal. Good night, Gunilla. Good night."

Gunilla kicked off her wooden shoes right by the place where harnesses and coats and wraps were hung. Jenny called out from the door, "Good night, Gunilla. Thanks for everything you did today."

The outer door opened and closed. A stream of cold air swept in all the way to the stalls.

But Jenny never stepped outside the door. Instead, she felt her way along to the arena door, which she had previously left half open. Nothing had been changed; there wasn't a sound anywhere as she let herself be engulfed by the darkness. She saw a light go off in the remotest quarter of the stalls. She heard Gunilla say something to a few of the horses. Then Gunilla trudged, with slow and heavy steps right past the entrance to the arena.

Her steps halted. Jenny held her breath. Gunilla must have wondered about the half-open door. She shut it with an angry bang.

Jenny sneaked over and put her ear against the keyhole. There now. Gunilla was farther and farther away. Click. She turned off the light switch. Something creaked loudly, emphatically. The door banged again. At last there came the heavy rattle of a large key being turned in a rusty lock.

Jenny remained there a few minutes silently, motionlessly. Carefully she peered through the keyhole, but she saw only utter darkness.

With a sigh of relief, she opened the door and stepped out into the stalls. As she passed those closest at hand, she sensed rather than saw that heads turned and surprised eyes tried to distinguish her figure. She stepped into the closest one, where Manilla was, and petted her on her hind quarters.

"Don't be afraid, now," she said in her softest, most tender voice. "It's just Jenny. I thought I'd stay here with you tonight."

CHAPTER 14

An Unexpected Solution

Jenny's watch verified the fact that scarcely five minutes
had passed before she went out to call for Lars. She knew
from experience how deceptive the passage of time could
be, especially when you were waiting alone in a state of
excitement. She would have to be absolutely certain that
Gunilla had had time to get out of sight.

Someone else was waiting excitedly and impatiently
—Lars. As soon as Jenny opened the door, the bushes in
the bend of the road came to life. A little figure flew from
out of the darkness and came running at top speed, close
to the walls of the stables. Jenny was pleased to note that
he avoided running across the middle of the snow-covered
yard.

"In with you!"

Lars tried desperately to distinguish Jenny's figure in
the darkness. He didn't need to worry. Even after what had
happened, his sister, to her surprise, felt something akin
to gratitude merely at feeling the pompom on his cap in
her hand and at hearing his excited whispers.

"Did everything go all right?"

"Perfectly. She didn't notice a thing. But, Lars, I have
made a most unpleasant discovery."

"What?"

"Here it is, completely dark, and naturally we don't dare to put on the lights. They would shine out over half of Nordvik. And I forgot to bring a flashlight with me. It won't be so nice to sit in the darkness all night long."

"But *I* didn't forget," Lars said with an almost world-weary maturity in his voice. "I brought with me that big flashlight I got for Christmas. New batteries and everything. Do I dare to turn it on?"

"Oh, how lucky, Lars. You're really great! No, don't turn it on yet. Hold on to my hand, and I'll try to keep you from falling into one of the water troughs. I thought that we could make a place for ourselves in the empty stall over there. It belongs to Tarantella, but she is an army horse and right now she's in service, you know. From there we can see the main entrance." Jenny stopped herself suddenly. But Lars had already heard, and there certainly was nothing wrong with his powers of observation. He picked it up in a flash.

"The main entrance? Why should we see that?"

Jenny hesitated. Then hastily she said, "Here we are. Now you can turn on the light. What a marvelous flashlight!"

"Great, isn't it?" Lars willingly admitted. "But what do you mean by saying that we have to be able to see the door?"

Jenny realized that there was no turning back. Once you had said "A" to Lars, the only thing to do was to continue with "B" and "C" and on through the rest of the alphabet.

"Here's a really nice horse blanket. Come on. Let's sit down. Now listen, Lars, I'm going to tell you something. We're not here simply because Rascal has hurt her leg, but because—well, wait, you can hear for yourself."

Jenny poured out the story quickly, in whispers, but with life and spark in every syllable, in every gesture. When Jenny got involved in something with all her might, not only her mouth moved, but also her eyes, eyebrows, and her hands.

They had placed the lamp on the blanket between them. It threw its light upward, making Lars's face pointed and angular. He resembled a small imp. His hair stood on end, and his eyes didn't wander from Jenny for so much as a split second.

When Jenny had finished, he nodded deeply, seriously. Then he began to look somewhat odd.

"It's just as I thought. Look, I know that it wasn't any elk!"

"Elk?" Jenny repeated without a flicker of comprehension.

Lars sputtered impatiently.

"Of course. Don't you remember that evening I sneaked out on account of The Secret Club? I told you and Mama afterwards. Of course, not absolutely everything was true, but I really did see that horse. I thought it looked like Rascal, but if I had said that, you would only have made fun of me. And I know it wasn't an elk, because I have seen elks at Skansen Zoo, and even here in Nordvik. It had a striped band on its forehead, and it was going along off to the side of the road, quiet and dignified. I saw it just for a couple of seconds, for that matter."

"Did you see who was in the saddle?" Jenny asked breathlessly. Miraculously enough, she didn't for a moment doubt Lars's truthfulness now.

Lars gazed down at the floor reflectively. He shook his head.

"It was going too fast, you see. I only remember the striped band on the forehead and—oh yes, it had a long tail. Perhaps the one who was riding had something red on. Yes, I think there was something red. There's a street light right near there."

"Keep talking, Lars," Jenny pleaded, stressing each word. "You say the person sitting on Rascal had on a red jacket. Oh, Lars. Think. Was it a boy or a girl? Think hard now, please, Lars! Big or little?"

But in spite of the fact that Lars thought so hard that he almost became pale from the strain, he couldn't remember one additional detail.

"I didn't *see* anything more," he replied sadly.

Still, Jenny felt aflame with a sort of triumph. At last there was someone who had seen the mysterious rider. It still had no face attached to it, but it was certainly redder than ever before.

Jenny, who had raised herself to her knees, remained in the stall for a while without moving. Then with great determination she got up and vigorously brushed off the knees of her trousers.

"Now let's make ourselves at home, Lars," she suggested. "And we aren't going to give up before we have caught that red ghost rider. Let's get out some food and eat. I'll go and get my bag—I put it in Rascal's stall. You can go after a few more horse blankets. They're on the shelf right beside the office door. Then we'll try to sleep for a few hours."

When Jenny came back, she was astonished at what she beheld—a real camp in the empty stall. The glaring, white light from the light revealed a meal as sumptuous in content as it was unique.

The dark horse blanket was a backdrop for a jar of honey, a pile of almonds, a ginger cookie in the shape of a pig—with two legs still intact—two onions, some sugar cubes, two turkey legs, a thick slice of ham with mustard on it, two cold boiled potatoes—on the point of collapse —and even a pickle.

"Have you ever seen anything so elegant?" Lars asked enthusiastically. He was just in the process of unpacking his wrinkled package of sandwiches.

"How could you manage to carry all this?" Jenny wondered aloud after she had had time to examine the astonishing "still life" that was to comprise their meal.

"Well, you know, my jacket has lots of pockets," he said proudly. "The mustard was the worst thing. But anyway, my sweater was already that color. Let's sit down."

Jenny sat down. What else could she do? Curiously enough her mouth had begun to water.

Lars slowly and deliberately unwrapped a mass of something—something quite odd both in color and consistency.

"What in the world do you have there?"

"Coconut cookies," said Lars with great satisfaction.

Jenny looked at them critically.

"Well, anyway, they *were* coconut cookies," she admitted at length.

"They can be packed very nicely," Lars said. "Mother always says that, remember. And the best thing about all this food," he continued, "is—do you know what it is?— well, it's that no one will ever miss any of these things."

"Hmmm," said Jenny contemplatively. "You're probably right. The turkey legs, perhaps. After all, they *are* pretty big."

"But they're so good!" Lars said as he examined the drumsticks lovingly. "There's one for each of us. And they have lots of meat on them, believe me. It was all that was left of the turkey. Nobody cares about these drumsticks. We ate most of the turkey on Christmas Day."

Jenny reflected that their mother would perhaps have had a different opinion. But she was hungry, and she put the idea right out of her mind.

"Here's my stuff," she said. "But of course it's nothing in comparison with yours."

Lars beamed with pleasure at Jenny's praise.

"Help yourself," he said generously.

Jenny recalled that the turkey had been marvelous on Christmas Day, but she couldn't believe that it had tasted as good then as it did right now. She confided this to Lars, and he didn't hesitate to agree.

"This tea you made is really good," he said.

When they had finished, Jenny was surprised to notice that even one of the onions had disappeared.

"It was strong, too," said Lars as he washed it down with

tea out of the cover of the Thermos. "I think I'll have a lit-tle honey. That will take away the taste. This was wonder-ful, Jenny. Wasn't it? And we didn't have to fuss with knives and forks. . . . You know, I really and truly feel sleepy."

He rolled himself up in a blanket in the corner of the stall. He stared woodenly, but contentedly, out into the surrounding darkness.

"Try to go to sleep now," Jenny said affectionately. "I will pick up the rest of the stuff. It's really not until tomor-row morning that we have to be on the alert."

Lars didn't answer. He was absolutely still.

While Jenny was throwing all the scraps into a sack and taking them to a garbage can near the back door, she began to collect her weary thoughts.

Try as she would, she couldn't help thinking about the complications that might arise if anyone discovered that Lars had sneaked out of the house. When he had first made his appearance out there on the road, she had been forced to make her decision with no hesitation. Now, as she ex-amined the situation more closely, she began to have her doubts. Her own absence during the night, she was posi-tive, would remain unnoticed. But Lars's—that was an-other matter.

In story books, such escapades usually come off with ex-traordinary success. Either they remain undiscovered, or else the authors of the books ignore the resultant worry and commotion back home.

Jenny recalled, with mounting uneasiness, how worried her mother was that night when Lars disappeared on his errand for The Secret Club. Suddenly she remembered that he now had a cold and, because of that, had been kept inside the house all day. What could be more natural than this—that one of her parents would go in and tuck him in during the course of the night? Dead silence from the nursery could be very suspicious.

Energetically she began to shake the blanket that had served as their tablecloth.

Jenny knew herself pretty well. She realized that the gnawing thought of what might happen at home if their absence were detected would not leave her a moment's peace during the many long hours that lay before her. It had been, and still was, her business to take the responsibility. She was older than Lars. She had sense enough to comprehend just what a night of wakefulness and anxiety could do to her parents.

She looked at Lars. There he was, rolled up in his horse blanket, his hair damp and tangled, his mouth half open, his bravery and boldness gone. He was merely a seven-year-old boy, subject to the most primitive instincts—hunger, thirst, weariness. In some respects he was similar to Rascal—a wonderful pal while things were happening, oftentimes a support in times of danger, but willing to let stronger ones bear the burdens of responsibility.

There was only one thing to do, and Jenny did it.

She grabbed the lamp and shot straight across the stable yard and up to the office. The key was still in the lock. She opened the door and went in.

Jenny began to analyze Viveca. True, she had a chilly disposition and a curt manner toward her younger brother and sisters, but when it came right down to it, Viveca could be a good comrade, even a warlike defender in critical situations. She didn't go out of her way to be amiable or considerate, but she was loyal. She saw everything in the cold, hard light of reality and behaved accordingly.

Jenny looked at her watch. Half-past ten. Mother and Dad wouldn't have had time to get home yet.

On the rickety, unvarnished desk, with its pitifully few items of business equipment, was a telephone. Jenny picked up the receiver and dialed her own telephone number.

There were several rings before anything happened. Then Viveca answered it by saying their number.

"Hi, Viveca. Are you ever going to be surprised. This is Jenny!"

It was important to use the right tone of voice. Smooth, but definite and decisive. She didn't have to fake the little tinge of breathless excitement in her voice, which emphasized the importance of what she had to say. The excitement came naturally and had already communicated itself to Viveca.

"I'm at the stables. I'm worried about Rascal, you know. I thought I would feel better if I could stay with her tonight. Do you understand?"

"Yeah," said Viveca. Her voice was utterly noncommittal. Was there any way of making older brothers and sisters understand?

"Nobody needs to know about this," Jenny said in her most positive voice.

A snort came through the telephone.

"Why are you calling, then?" said Viveca, without any expression whatsoever.

"Because Lars followed me. He's here now and has decided he is going to stay, come what may. You know what he's like."

"Silly kid!" The two simple words were fraught with meaning.

Jenny continued. She spoke slowly and emphatically to give her sister time to absorb the full, sensational value of her news.

"He's been pretty clever about everything at home. Fixed it so that nobody would notice anything. Messed up the bedcovers and everything. And now he's out cold. Snug and warm and sleeping like a log. As far as I'm concerned, it's O.K. if he stays, and I promise to smuggle him home early in the morning. But I won't have a moment's peace, you understand, because if Mother and Dad discover that he's gone, they'll be absolutely horrified. For that reason I thought it was best to let you in on it. Here we are, and there's nothing we need. But if no one notices, you certainly don't need to say anything, huh?"

So much was at stake at this very moment. There was dead silence for a few seconds. Then back came Viveca's answer.

"He's crazy, that kid. So are you both, if you want my opinion. You think you can do just as you please. But O.K. I'll keep it to myself. Cover up so you won't freeze. Besides, Lars has a cold."

"O.K., sure. We have piles of blankets."

Jenny's voice gave no hint of the tremendous relief that came over her like a shower. She probably had had a pretty good idea that it would turn out this way—that Viveca had not yet declared herself on the side of the adults, and that, in spite of all, she was still a sister.

"This is really good of you, Viveca," she said in her calmest voice. "I'll take care of Lars, I promise. 'Bye now."

"Enjoy yourselves. Bye-bye."

When Jenny returned to join Lars, she found that he had stretched out on his back, all tension gone and sleep and rest permeating every limb. She had brought back some additional blankets from the big pile. She squatted down and untied Lars's boots and removed them. He sighed and sniffled in his sleep. As she put an additional blanket on him, his lips moved in a long, incoherent mumble.

Jenny remembered that Lars talked quite a bit in his sleep, especially when he had a cold. She bent over him and listened. At first she heard only a series of inarticulate sounds, but gradually these sounds began to become words.

"The Bear! The Bear has the puck!"

Obviously he carried international ice hockey with him even in the realm of his subconscious. And totally unexpectedly, Lars raised up his head so violently that he almost bumped Jenny in the face and screamed in his shrillest voice, "Offside! Offside!"

Once again his head fell down on the blanket. The horses, aroused by his screams, were moving restlessly in the nearby stalls. Jenny sank down beside Lars. She chortled quietly to herself. The events of the day had beyond a doubt fired Lars's ever vivid imagination up to the boiling point.

Her laugh, however, was suffocated by a big yawn. Everything—the sight of Lars who had resumed his peaceful slumber; the muffled noises of the stall growing dimmer and dimmer; the comforting knowledge that Viveca was aware of their whereabouts—contributed to the fact that even Jenny was able to relax. Sleep came rolling and spread itself out over her just like a thick, soft, downy comforter. She stared vacantly up at the uncertain darkness in the beams of the roof. Lars's face was right next to her own. It had a clean, ivory sheen in the light from the flashlight.

Jenny stretched out her hand and moved the tips of her fingers along his soft chin. It was comforting and cheering to have him so near. With one hand she felt along the side of the flashlight until she found the switch and turned it off.

Now the stall seemed overwhelming and all-encompassing—it was like a giant's throat. She had a sensation of falling down, down—deeper, deeper.

Just as Jenny was about to slide over the threshold of deep sleep, she came to very violently. Something was moving easily, cautiously, right by her feet.

She didn't have time to become thoroughly frightened; the intruder revealed himself. The stable cat! He found his way along Jenny's legs, agreeably surprised at finding this treasure in the empty stall. She could feel him settling down and seeking support for his back against the hollow behind her knees. Now the harmony of the stall was complete; the last instrument had been added.

The cat purred. Jenny fell asleep.

What was that? A murmur out of Lars, a snort from one of the horses, a movement of the cat? Jenny didn't have time to seek out the cause. But she was wide awake in the course of just a few seconds.

How long had she slept? It seemed as if an eternity of unconsciousness were behind her. She sat up to feel for the flashlight so quickly that she overturned it. The darkness was more impenetrable than she had remembered before she fell asleep. Now, at last! Here was the switch. Light!

Without even thinking, she was on her feet. Had she overslept? Had the unwelcome guest already arrived?

The powerful light penetrated the darkness mercilessly, seeking out the far corners of the stall, proceeding on toward the stable entrance. Everything was as it should be. With a reproachful glance at Jenny, the cat shifted over to the crook of Lars's arm, where he resumed his rudely interrupted nap.

Jenny looked at her watch. Five o'clock! How lucky that she had awakened. Just to be on the safe side, she resolved to take a quick, quiet tour of inspection.

A whinny from one corner of the stable greeted both Jenny and the beginning of a new day. She couldn't make out which one of the horses was so wide awake. None of the others, however, showed any intention of neighing in response.

Rascal stood with her nose in the water trough. The

water was disappearing surprisingly quickly, but utterly silently. Jenny didn't dare to linger with her—now was the time to be more alert than ever. But hastily she bent down and directed the light so that it would shine on the ailing fetlock and would enable her to see if it had become more swollen during the night. It looked as slender and flexible as ever. Relieved, Jenny straightened up.

As she did this, a beam of light hit a corner of the stall that was otherwise quite dark. All the way under the crib, in a niche over in the corner near the wall, she could see something yellowish. Jenny leaned over mechanically and stuck her hand in the corner. As she did so, a square object fell out.

Holding it in her hand, she could see that it was a common red and yellow cardboard box that had at one time contained candy. On the cover, printed in slanting letters, was the single word, RASCAL.

Her surprise mounting, she opened the box. She folded back the tissue paper and, a second later, took out something that, at first glance, resembled a rather crude piece of leather.

She let it slide slowly through her fingers and, upon closer examination, found that it was anything but crude. It was a nose band of the softest white, woolly lambskin, painstakingly fashioned and lined with white flannel. At one time she herself had considered making something like this for Rascal's bridle, but she hadn't really believed that she could be that clever with her hands.

Fascinatedly, Jenny stared at the small, fine stitches along the edge. Shutting her eyes, she could almost see the hand that had done this lovely stitching; she could almost feel the presence of another person, the presence of the "outside influence"; she could identify herself with this person's apprehensions and temptations.

Quiet! What was that? Wasn't there a noise over there toward the entrance? Or had one of the horses made a sound?

Quick as a flash, Jenny turned off the light. In total darkness she carefully put the leather band in the box, bent down, and returned it to its hiding place.

Silently Jenny crept out of Rascal's stall and started along the passage. She couldn't decide if the thing that had just frightened her was real or not. But she knew that the unidentified secret rider—if he or she would come at all —might come at any moment. She no longer dared to have the light on.

Her eyes had not yet had enough time to become accustomed to the thick darkness all around her. As is usual in such situations, everything had gotten out of proportion. How long, really, *was* the stall passage? Had she been moving terribly quickly or terribly slowly? Best to inch her way along until she could feel the wall of the stalls. How far away could it be, anyhow?

She felt as if she had landed in the middle of a coal-black vacuum. Still, the wall must be just a few inches away. Or, at most, an arm's length. She held one hand out protectingly in front of her; in the other hand she held the lamp.

Ah! At last. A wall, a corner, an empty stall, another wall. This must be Manilla's stall. Eight, ten more steps.

Here was the office wall. If she could hide herself in there with the door open just an inch or so, she could see through the slit and have a good view of the outside door. The person she was waiting for might possibly have a flashlight that could, of course, light up that part of the stall all at once. Jenny knew that she didn't want to be taken by surprise without time to gather her wits after the secret visitor's identity had been revealed. That would be the most difficult moment. Well, no use thinking about that now. She simply had to concentrate and keep herself under control.

This was easier said than done. Jenny heard her own panting breaths. Just like the moments following a strenuous gallop.

Momentarily she stationed herself in her hiding place. No longer was the darkness so impenetrable. The veils seemed to lift themselves from the surroundings, thin layer by layer. From her vantage point she could make out the dim contours of the nearby stalls. A stall door, painted light gray, showed up unmistakably a little farther away. Suddenly there was a prolonged murmur, and a sneeze—unmistakably masculine in origin. Jenny jumped. Lars! She had forgotten all about him in these last exciting moments. Should she wake him up so that he could be in on the solution to the mystery? He had really earned it . . .

But a second later Jenny knew that it was too late. She wouldn't have time to waken Lars.

A weak sound, but one that was easily recognizable, penetrated the boards of the wall—a typical sound around Nordvik in the winter: the dry muffled squeak of footsteps in the snow. And so close to the door! Jenny held her breath.

A key scraped against the wood and the metal—once, twice. Now it found its mark. There was a heavy rattling. Unconsciously Jenny manipulated her right hand, as if it were she herself who was holding the old, heavy key—she herself who was turning it in the lock.

In addition, there were the usual sounds of the stalls. The movement of hoofs, the snorts, the rustle of straw.

Over near the door there was a ribbon of reddish light. Noiselessly, the door was opening—little by little, wider, wider. A tiny draft of fresh air shot across the expanse, all the way to Jenny's hiding place.

Now the door had opened sufficiently to accommodate a thin person. A very thin person. The figure emerged. Medium height. Breathlessly, Jenny tried to see into the shadows.

Then, without any previous warning, something happened that made it seem as if the horses, the stalls, everything were going to explode. From the farthest part of the stable came a sound that mysteriously seemed to crack open the night and split the darkness in pieces.

"Hey, Tumba! Shoot. Shoot! Sho-o-o-o-o-ot!"

There was a chalk-white flurry of snow near the door as it slammed shut.

For a split second Jenny stood as if she had been turned to stone. Then the office door flew open. It hit the wooden walls with a crash as Jenny crossed the width of the passage in just two giant steps.

She managed to catch only a glimpse of a dark figure, in

pants, sharply contrasted against the whiteness outside. As she slipped on the steps, she saw something moving in the bushes down near the pasture. But when Jenny had regained her balance, whatever it was had disappeared. She knew that someone must be running down in that direction, and she hurried, like a person possessed, along the clear tracks across the stable yard. The last trace of the moving figure was the sound of branches being broken over in the corner of the meadow, and a falling plank down at the place where the children had made a small hole in the fence. Finally, Jenny sensed more than heard or saw that the figure had been swallowed up by the woods farther away.

"Stop!" Jenny screamed. "Stop. Don't you hear? You! Stop, I said."

But the only answer was the weak whisper from the desolate treetops.

There was a noise behind Jenny. Quickly she turned around. There in the stall door stood the astonished Lars in his stocking feet, with an old horse blanket wrapped around him and trailing on the ground.

"Did he run away?" he asked as he gasped for breath in the frosty air.

"He or she," Jenny answered a little bitterly. "Why did you think you had to make such a lot of noise? And just at that particular time?"

"I made a noise?"

"Yes. You screamed at the top of your lungs for Tumba to shoot, or something just as idiotic," Jenny said, her bitterness mounting.

"I woke up because someone was screaming so horribly," Lars admitted contemplatively. "Just imagine. It was me!"

Jenny looked at him. She was aware that disappointment, anger, and a strong desire to laugh were fighting a terrific battle within her. The battle was short and almost one-sided. Lars looked just too comical. And the moment she had waited for—and feared—the hardest moment of all, wouldn't have to occur this morning.

She went over to Lars, lifted him under his arms, and swung him around completely.

"Come on, now," she said gently. "We'll clean up everything here and say good night, I mean good morning, to Rascal. In any case, one thing is certain. No ghost is going to try to ride her today. And Lars—can you imagine anything nicer right this minute than the clean, white sheets?"

"No," said Lars with a large, engulfing yawn. "Yes, I can too. A pillow."

CHAPTER 15

The Hardest Moment of All

That afternoon, as Jenny sat curled up in a corner of the sofa, killing time by reading a book on the care of horses, Mariann telephoned. Jenny answered the phone with little enthusiasm; the far from peaceful night, her fitful sleep among the horse blankets, and the journey home in the raw cold of the morning had all contributed to making her a little chilly and out of sorts for the rest of the day.

To be sure, everything had gone a good deal better than she had expected. Their nocturnal adventure had remained undetected, and both Lars and Jenny, feeling that it was almost too good to be true, had willingly tumbled into bed and slept far into the morning. But the chill had remained with her, and stiffness had entered her body and showed no intention of going away. Even Lars was quiet and subdued. The international ice hockey match seemed to have been forgotten completely, and at the moment he lay on his side on the floor playing absent-mindedly with a toy crane. His sense of guilt for the failure of the previous night's vigil had begun to weigh heavily on his conscience, and his glances at Jenny wavered between sadness and remorse.

For once Viveca had displayed her nicest side and had exuberantly told how she had acquitted herself when her parents came home.

"A mere trifle," she said with an air of superiority. "You don't need to think that it is just you and Lars who can fix things up. Mother was worried, of course, and wanted to go in and have a look at Lars, but I simply said, 'Don't go in there, for heaven's sake. He's sleeping like a log,' which was quite true. You had told me this just a few minutes before. The fact that he was up at the stable and not at home was of no importance."

No, Jenny had to admit that she and Lars had been lucky . . . in everything except the most important matter. When she heard Mariann's pleasant, friendly voice, it occurred to her that here at last was someone to whom she could confide her troubles. Someone who knew horses, knew the riding academy well, knew their friends there.

"Hi, Jenny."

"Hi, yourself."

"How's everything with you these days?"

"Oh, just about the same."

"It seems like forever since we got together and talked," said Mariann hesitantly, obviously groping for words.

"I know. It's a shame, but Rascal takes so much of my time, and I never do see you at the stables."

"Well, when you aren't allowed to ride, there's. . . . But listen, Jenny. Can you come over here for a while? I'm all alone at home, and there's something I want to talk to you about."

"Yes, I guess I can. Should I come right away?"

"Sure. I'll put on some water for tea and fix us something to eat. See you soon."

During the time Jenny was taking a short cut through Nordvik, she began to reflect that Mariann had really sounded awfully eager. Usually her manner was calm and her speech tended to be somewhat slow. But probably she wanted to make the most of the opportunity now that her family was away. Jenny remembered the fact that Mariann's mother was the sort who was always in evidence, and she liked to be on friendly terms with her daughter and her classmates. That was nice for a little while, but naturally the girls liked to be by themselves. Therefore, up to this time, they had been at Jenny's house almost always whenever they had been together.

It is curious how little effort is required for two people to become strangers—two people who have previously had almost daily contact. Naturally, Jenny and Mariann had seen each other at school, but Mariann's curt and brusque manner had caused Jenny to avoid her lately. She had to admit that she had deliberately avoided Mariann the last time. Of course, it was easy to understand why Mariann had no desire to renew the memories of the time when she too had ridden.

All too quickly, Jenny found herself outside Mariann's gate. Suddenly, bitterly, she regretted her decision to come. It would never do, now, to take Mariann into her confidence as she had done before—least of all when the matter concerned Rascal.

The granite gateposts looked harsh and uninviting. On

one of them was fastened a polished copper plate with the name "Lidman" on it. Everything about Mariann and her home was so well-polished and nicely cared for that Jenny felt a little envious. There were no beaten-up bicycles or doll buggies cluttering up the walk or the steps, no baseball bats or ski poles unexpectedly tumbling down out of dark closets and scaring a visitor half out of his wits. Everything inside was just as precise and tasteful as the brick exterior that the house presented to the outside world.

Jenny shut the gate behind her and haltingly went up the walk from which all traces of snow had been removed.

The door opened before she even got to it.

"I saw you through the window," Mariann explained.

The hallway was not very large, but its marble floor glistened. While Mariann helped Jenny take off her jacket and silently hung it on a velvet-covered hanger, Jenny realized, with a sinking feeling, just how estranged they had really become.

Had they been adults, they would no doubt have made some small talk about how long it had been since they had met. But there was only deep silence until Mariann said abruptly, "Shall we sit in the living room or up in my room?"

"In your room," Jenny suggested. She continued, more or less to break the ice, "I think it's so nice up there."

"O.K., come on up."

Was that awful, inexplicable silence going to return?

Jenny needn't have been concerned. Very hastily, Mariann said, "How is Rascal?"

Jenny looked at her in amazement. She saw that Mariann's cheeks were very pink, and immediately she knew: Mariann regrets this whole business. Basically she has always been all right. Now all at once she's trying to tell me that we can talk about horses just as we used to and that she doesn't entirely begrudge my owning Rascal.

"Rascal's fine. Well, she does have a little sprain, but I'm sure that will be O.K. in just a couple of days."

They looked at each other. Invisible walls seemed to rise. Then a breath of spring touched the frozen fields.

"What did you get for Christmas?"

Having said this, Jenny immediately felt so much happier and more at ease that she hopped up onto Mariann's elegant studio couch, drawing her legs up under her. "Tell me. I want to see."

Mariann showed her. A pair of light green slippers with swansdown linings, a matching light green suitcase trimmed with darker leather, an alarm clock in a green leather case, and all sorts of accessories in almost the same color—a color so reminiscent of spring.

Jenny, beaming, said, "Oh, they're lovely!" And she meant it.

Mariann put the suitcase back in the closet.

"Maybe I'll get to take a trip to England in the summer for an intensive English course," she said. "You see, this is some sort of consolation prize—now that my parents don't have the expense of my riding lessons." Her tone of voice betrayed nothing. Nothing, that is, other than monumental self-control, so unobtrusive that it was almost invisible. Still, Jenny knew that self-control was definitely being exercised, because she knew Mariann very well.

For her own sake, Jenny decided to change the subject. It was no fun to be with Mariann when it was like this. She kicked her own shoes under the bed and said, "Look, you said there was something special you wanted to talk to me about."

It seemed that Mariann didn't hear. She was busy in the closet.

"I got a new dress too, but I had been down with Mother to try it on, so it wasn't actually a surprise. Do you like it?"

She held up the new dress for Jenny to see. It was light blue—the latest style, with a short, pleated skirt.

Jenny had always been of the opinion that Mariann dressed simply and well. Her blouses and sweaters, slacks, and jackets were never elaborate. They always seemed modest and comfortable, utterly in keeping with Mariann's calm and poised personality. Jenny observed that, while this dress was nice and in good taste, the style of it was so utterly new, so fashionable, that it really was showy. Mariann had suddenly become fashion-conscious, and Jenny felt the chasm between them growing wider. Tension mounted so quickly that Jenny became a little worried. Then she said sincerely, "Oh, it's so neat and nice. And you look so good in blue."

Again there was silence. They both looked at the dress, avoiding each other's eyes.

"I'll go down and get the tea," said Mariann. "Here's the dress if you'd like to look at it. When you're finished, please hang it in my closet. There's a new skirt hanging there too, if you'd like to see it. I'll be right back."

She disappeared. For a few seconds Jenny stood there

with the light blue dress mutely suspended from its hanger. Clothes themselves can be quite eloquent between girls, but not this dress. It simply hung.

Doubtfully, Jenny began to let her thoughts wander into unfamiliar territory as she walked slowly over to the closet's half-open door. With a sudden impatient movement she jerked it all the way open.

The opening of the door created a momentary draft. Along with this draft came a smell so strong and pungent that Jenny nearly backed away. The smell of horses!

Jenny had to smile. That smell lingers. It certainly doesn't go away in any hurry. She let her eyes wander among the garments, and up on the shelves. No wonder the closet smelled. There was Mariann's crash helmet, just where it had always been. Right next to it were the riding gloves—Mariann's practical brown gloves—and the heavy striped woolen muffler, which she was using even back as far as the time when they were both in the beginners' group. Jenny hung up the blue dress and took down the muffler. Fantastic how the smell refused to go away! Pretty soon the new dress would smell too. Jenny giggled.

And there was the new skirt—straight, narrow, moss-green. Even the skirt was ultra-stylish. And next to it was something red, something short.

Mechanically Jenny pushed apart the hangers. There was a red parka with a white lining in the hood.

Jenny stood very still. Her fingertips played idly with the zipper. Quickly she bent forward.

Yes, even it smelled of horses. Terribly much so. But of course there was no smell in the world so unique as this.

Jenny constantly had to listen to comments concerning that smell, both at home and in school. Moreover, Viveca never used the word "smell." She used the word "stink" instead, and she said it whenever she came anywhere near Jenny's closet.

Jenny couldn't recall ever having seen Mariann in the red parka. There was no escaping the fact that the smell of horses could linger in garments for months. Either that, or the jacket could prove . . .

Jenny pushed the hangers together and shut the closet door. In order to put a stop to this disquieting train of thought, she did an about-face and ambled over to the desk.

You couldn't compare this one with Jenny's weather-beaten desk, just as you couldn't compare Jenny's ponderous handwriting with the elegant, fine printing on the covers of Mariann's blue composition books. "Mariann Lidman. English Dictation." "Mariann Lidman. German Vocabulary."

Absently, Jenny leafed through some of the pages. Was it even remotely possible that Mariann, who had among the highest grades in the class, would sit here studying, even during the Christmas vacation? It looked suspiciously like it. Jenny's conscience began to annoy her. She had almost forgotten her own disgraceful grade in Composition. Everything else had been pushed aside in favor of Rascal's ailment.

Something else caught her eye. A little enamel object, in the shape of a filly, lay in the pencil tray. Jenny picked it up only to discover that it was a pencil sharpener. Did it really work? Right near it was a pencil with a broken point.

Jenny looked around in search of the scrap basket. Every-thing in the room was so clean and tidy; it would' never do to mess it up. There it was—under the desk. Small, neat, made out of blue plastic.

Jenny slowly rotated the pencil in the sharpener. Yes, it really worked. The shavings came out in long strips and slowly fell down into the basket. It seemed almost a shame to dirty the wastebasket. But wait! It wasn't completely empty. There in the bottom were a few slips of paper and some other white scraps.

Jenny stiffened. Without looking up, she replaced the pencil sharpener. The pencil landed, with a clatter, right beside it. She leaned forward, staring at the contents of the wastebasket. Then she reached down and brought up one of the white scraps.

The plastic of the basket felt cold and hard as her hand touched it. But what she held in her hand was warm, soft, and smooth.

She straightened up. She couldn't take her eyes from the piece of leather. Then she laid it on the desk and let her fingertips travel slowly back and forth over its woolly sur-face.

From the stairs she could hear heavy steps—the steps so characteristic of a slight person carrying a heavy tray. She heard the rattle of the dishes and the turning of the door-knob as Mariann tried—unsuccessfully a couple of times —to open the door. Yet she stood there motionless, with her hand over the piece of leather. She felt that she didn't want to do anything about all this at the moment. Instead she would simply let things happen as they might. There were times when that was the best thing to do. No use in forcing the issue. In the long run, things that happen naturally have more power than events that are carefully, calculatedly manipulated.

Jenny had no idea what sort of expression she had on her face. She felt as if there were no expression at all. But in any case, Mariann must have caught on. There she stood, like a statue, holding the tray. She directed her gaze to the thing that Jenny was studying so intently—the piece of leather.

Jenny was still fondling it softly.

"Well, of course, it's too late now. You'll probably never believe me. But this was what I wanted to talk to you about. I was only postponing it for a little while, but I swear that I intended to tell you everything before you left."

"This morning in Rascal's stall I found the box with the nose band in it," said Jenny, surprised that her voice sounded so normal. She was even more surprised to hear herself saying, "Thank you for making such a nice nose band for Rascal. She must look great with it on."

At that point Mariann became red as a beet. Jenny had never seen her like that before. Flushed, pink, yes—but never beet-red.

She must have sensed the extent of her embarrassment herself, because she suddenly put both hands over her face and went and sat on the bed.

"Forgive me, Jenny," she said in a muffled voice. "Forgive me. It was a terrible, awful thing. . . . And the worst of it was I was so terribly envious of you and Rascal. But

. . . well, Jenny, this is no excuse. I don't mean it to be
one. But have you ever tried to live without riding?"

Jenny sat down on the stool beside the desk. She turned
around so that she faced Mariann. In her hand she still
held the piece of leather, but now her fist was clenched as
if she had gotten hold of something she was reluctant to
release. She thought to herself: "Live without riding? It

sounds dramatic and silly. I lived perfectly well before I ever sat on a horse. But now! I have to try and understand the full meaning of these words. Live . . . get up and get dressed . . . go to school . . . eat . . . live with my parents, Lars, Mona, and Viveca . . . but no Rascal, no stable . . ."

She said at length, "I'll be glad if I never have to go through that experience."

Mariann folded her hands across her knees. She continued.

"It's sheer agony. You do try. You go to school. You even study during vacation. You try on clothes. You think of the summer vacation and try to look forward to it. No, that isn't so. You can't try to look forward to something. Either you look forward to it or you don't. And every time you take the train, you go right by the riding academy. Whenever you go to school or to the library, you see the stables at the end of the road. It's completely hopeless."

"Then it was you this morning," Jenny said. She had to come back to the subject—to get used to the idea.

Mariann looked down at the floor.

"It was then that I decided," she said. "When you ran after me and screamed 'Stop!' I realized right then and there that it was you I was deceiving. Stealing from, you might even say. Not a stranger who just happened to have the great fortune of owning Rascal, but you, Jenny. I saw you, heard you, and I knew at once that you were desperately worried. I didn't want that to happen. When I ran across the meadow, I knew for certain that I had to talk with you."

"Why did you pick on Rascal in particular?" Jenny mumbled. "There are so many horses at the stables. You could have taken a different one every single day. Didn't it ever occur to you that Rascal might have gotten over-worked? She was tired a lot of times."

Mariann raised her head and stared at Jenny.

"You ask why. Why did I choose Rascal? You chose her yourself from among many others. You know perfectly well. There simply isn't another horse like Rascal."

Jenny was silent. She poked at the pencil sharpener and hung the piece of leather on its back like a saddle. Mariann observed her intently and continued, this time in a less agitated voice.

"One thing, Jenny. I was terribly careful with her. Careful and affectionate. And she likes me, you know. One morning she neighed at me."

"At me, too," Jenny started to say. But she didn't say it. An unreasonable sense of indignation, a poisonous feeling, was starting to well up inside her. Rascal is mine! Mine! Not yours! But then Jenny saw the light again. Her indignation disappeared. Discussion of all this would lead to nothing. It might be hard to explain, but somehow, in some crazy way, Rascal would seem to be less her own if she had said, "She neighed at me, too."

Instead she hopped up from the stool and went over and sat down beside Mariann.

"I know that she likes you. She goes crazy over every red jacket she sees. It was because of her fascination with red jackets that I began to suspect that someone else was riding her."

Jenny related the entire story of Rascal's strange escapades and of her even stranger passion for Cecilia Acker. The more the story progressed, the less tense the situation was.

"But you never suspected me," said Mariann with a hint of bewilderment in her voice. Her head was up now, but some of the redness was still streaking her light complexion. Her white-blond hair fell evenly down on her neck, but around her temples there were small curls clinging to her damp forehead.

"No. That idea never occurred to me. The one I suspected was Bengt. He has been acting so funny, you see. Even now—now that I know it was you—I still think that Bengt has been behaving pretty peculiarly of late."

Mariann nodded.

"I think I know why. Look, it isn't completely impossible that Bengt is suspicious too—that he suspects me. One morning I dawdled a little too long in the stall—I think I even forgot to clean one hoof, because I suddenly looked at the clock and saw how late it was. Just as I was rushing down the road, Bengt came. I think perhaps he saw me, even though I sneaked into some bushes. Probably he didn't want to tell on me because I think he feels sorry for me."

"And he probably didn't think it was much fun to see me so mystified, either," Jenny said. She had been very cautious when she made this statement, but Mariann blinked anyway. Jenny continued hastily, "But of course everyone has heard so many stories about Bengt that it's no wonder I began to suspect him. I feel sorry for him."

Jenny's voice had a faraway sound. In reality, it wasn't Bengt she was thinking about. She was thinking of someone for whom she felt even sorrier.

"Listen," she said resolutely. "Pour the tea and let's drink up. And while we're having something to eat, please tell me why in the world you aren't allowed to ride any more. That sprain you got was nothing serious. And you were on the way to being an expert. Jumping, drill, everything. Everybody says the same."

Mariann poured the tea mechanically, as if she were grateful for any attention that was paid her. She handed Jenny a cup of tea and passed her some sugar and some pastries. Jenny noticed that Mariann's hands were shaking. When Mariann observed that Jenny had noticed this, her hands stopped shaking.

Jenny understood about Mariann's self-control, but this was carrying things too far. She glowered—at nothing in particular—and bit angrily into a sweet roll.

"Tell me," she almost commanded. "You've got to."

"It's Mother," said Mariann, biting into her own sweet roll, not as furiously as Jenny had, but slowly, with resignation. "Papa couldn't care less, actually. He just keeps saying that I shouldn't make Mother worried but should go along with what she says. She's scared stiff of anything to do with horses. Her brother—she had only one—had an accident when he was riding one time, you see, and he was thrown off and hit a huge rock. He didn't have a crash helmet on."

"Oh, that's what it's all about," said Jenny, much subdued. "Then, of course, I suppose you have to try and understand." She took a huge gulp from her cup of tea. Then she said, "You *can* understand, but something like that shouldn't be allowed to ruin someone else's life. The argument doesn't really hold water. Not for a whole lifetime, anyway."

She glanced at Mariann out of the corner of her eye. There she sat, voiceless, motionless. She had always been pretty quiet and had sat pretty still in the classroom too.

"Just imagine," said Jenny. "Think how nice everything might have been if you were still allowed to ride. I almost flunked composition, you know, and as for math—well the teacher has almost given me up in despair. I must study more—I've simply got to. But then I get to thinking about the stables and about Rascal who wants to get out and about the sun shining. And the ice, and everything else. I just don't have time for everything. You could have been a big help to me, riding her a couple of mornings a week, or something like that."

"Don't even talk about it," Mariann pleaded. "I don't want to hear any more. I'll go out of my mind. Certainly, I won't be doing it on the sly any more. I mean, I just couldn't do it now unless they knew about it at home. I really don't like sneaky things. If you could have known—when I saw you in school sometimes. You wouldn't understand, I'm sure, because you've never done anything like this. But it was awful."

Jenny put her half-eaten roll back on the plate. For a few minutes she merely stared into space. Many times she had imagined herself in one situation or another. She had also imagined that she would know how to handle this or that problem. She would know just what was right, and she would behave accordingly, without hesitation. No looking sideways, no letting herself be hampered by dread, shyness, indecision. There was complete freedom in the realm of the imagination.

Now, here before her, a fine opportunity loomed. An opportunity that left no doubt about what was the right and proper thing to do. An opportunity to prove that she didn't fear reproach or censure.

Her mouth was dry as a desert. Reality was not quite as she had conceived it in her fantasy. Fear was very much with her. But censure—had there ever been anything that could not be doubted—not be criticized? In any event, fear *could* be driven out the door.

"Mariann," she said, "I am going to go and talk with your mother. I'm going to tell her just how it is—no, naturally not the fact that you've been riding Rascal in secret, but everything else. About how you feel about riding, and what it means to you to ride. Anyway, I can try."

Mariann stared at her in dumb amazement.

"You can't do that," she said. "You don't dare. I appreciate the thought, Jenny, but you aren't the kind who can talk to Mother."

"Maybe not, but I can at least pretend that I am," said Jenny stubbornly, as she gave a little sigh.

Mariann still looked just as doubtful of the whole thing.

"You don't know my mother. She's really a nice person, but there are some things that you just can't get her to discuss. Jenny, it won't do any good."

"Regardless of that, I will have tried. Right now I feel

as if I could do it, so I guess it's best to get it over with as soon as possible," Jenny said loudly. To herself she thought: "If I think about it long enough, I'll talk myself out of it." Her thoughts wandered to Rascal, as if they could somehow find comfort there. Oh to be with her instead of with these stupid, uncomprehending people. "Oh, yes, you did tell me. Your mother isn't home."

"I heard the door just now," Mariann admitted with great hesitation. "But, Jenny . . ."

"Now is the time," said Jenny firmly.

And so it was that she hurried through the door—this girl who had recognized her duty and who intended to carry it through.

Mrs. Lidman was standing near the hall closet taking off her leather-lined overshoes. Perhaps it was lucky that Jenny appeared so unexpectedly that Mrs. Lidman really didn't have time to feel that she was alone.

"Hello," Jenny said as she curtsied and remained standing in the doorway. All at once she plunged in, well aware that she was purposely saying something irrevocable. "I'd like to . . . may I talk to you about something, Mrs. Lidman?"

"Well. It's Jenny, isn't it?" she said, offering her hand. "And how are you, my friend? Nothing has happened to Mariann, has it?"

The latter sentence came out a little breathlessly. Jenny felt that she had perhaps started off on the wrong foot.

"Oh, no, of course not. She's sitting up there in her room, drinking tea. But . . ."

"You really frightened me there for a moment. Now come in and sit down."

Mrs. Lidman led the way and sat down on the semicircular gray couch in the living room. She was a small person. Her narrow feet were trim and neat in the high-heeled shoes that she wore. Her skin, like her whole figure, seemed thin and transparent. Jenny was conscious of her dark and friendly eyes—close-set just like Mariann's.

Jenny perched on the edge of an easy chair. After all, she was only thirteen, and she hadn't really had the time to think out what she was going to say. At first she was silent. Then she said, "Well, Mrs. Lidman . . ."

"Aunt Marie," said Mariann's mother. "You and Mariann are such good friends. Call me Aunt Marie. And you needn't be at all uneasy. I am—or, I should say, have been —rather shy myself."

Jenny now saw the picture more clearly. She said, "It's about Mariann. Don't think I am silly. Even if I am, I've got to say what I'm going to say. Mariann's not like she used to be."

An expression of grave doubt spread over Mrs. Lidman's face, but Jenny didn't look away, even for a moment. She simply had to get this business off her chest, come what may. She moistened her lips.

"Mariann is bored. Not just bored. She's unhappy. Really, truly unhappy, and it's going to get worse. She's pretty much by herself at school. She hasn't even once wanted to talk to me—not before now. She just can't go on like this. You've got to let her ride again."

Now it had been said aloud. Had Jenny looked at herself in the mirror she would have been astonished. Her skin was ashen, and her eyes were dark and somber.

Mariann's mother didn't move a muscle. Her hands were stretched out stiffly against the dark upholstery of the couch. She had nothing to say.

Jenny went on.

"Mariann didn't want me to say anything. I think it's pretty horrible myself when people meddle in things that are none of their business, but I felt . . . I thought. . . . Well, my mother doesn't always know how I feel about everything. Therefore, I thought if I could explain . . ."

They looked at each other seriously. Mrs. Lidman said, "I think you're very nice and awfully sweet. But do you know why I keep Mariann from riding?"

"I know. Mariann told me. That was a terrible thing, and I'm terribly sorry it happened. But there is nobody in the whole riding academy who can ride like Mariann. That's a fact! Why does it need to be like this—with her not being allowed to do the very thing she is so well suited for? She could just as easily be run over by a car, or get hit in the head with a big icicle, or any number of things. I mean, you could have almost anything in the world happen to you—things you've never dreamed of, things you couldn't possibly prevent, even if you never again rode a horse."

"Don't you believe," Mrs. Lidman asked, "don't you believe that she will get over it? There is so much else that she could do—travel, have a good time. And she's very interested in her studies at school. With every promotion in school there will be more things that will fill up her time."

Jenny shook her head.

"She won't get over it. Maybe when she's really grown up—I don't know. But not now. Pretty soon she'll stop being interested in her studies, too, because she thinks nothing is fun any more."

Jenny's last statement had been especially well chosen. Jenny could tell that herself. Sometimes you're just lucky in finding the precise words. Simple and self-explanatory, but the very words that make clear exactly what you are trying to say.

The words were not lost on Mariann's mother. As yet, her hands remained stretched out on the edge of the couch. Jenny suddenly realized that this woman was the source of Mariann's self-control. She wondered how she would have reacted had she been the adult who was facing this girl named Jenny.

"You shouldn't think too badly of me," said Mariann's mother calmly. "When I knew that she was out riding. . . . You probably can't understand how a mother feels about these things. But I never could stop thinking that something was going to happen."

"Nothing is going to happen to Mariann," Jenny said consolingly. She began to smile for the first time during their conversation. "She is very, very careful and sensible and everything else."

"You're quite right. She doesn't think anything is fun any more," said Mrs. Lidman, still deep in thought. "I'm aware of that. A mother does notice some things, too, you know."

Jenny was about to blurt out, "But then why doesn't a

mother *do* something?" Luckily she stopped herself. Mariann's mother was the type of adult who moved very, very slowly. Jenny thought to herself, "Just hold your tongue. Be quiet." She had said what she had to say.

She calculated correctly. Mrs. Lidman wanted to say something.

"She is unhappy, just as you say," she remarked. "And it's almost worse for me to see her that way than to stay here at home and be worried. Yes, it *is* worse. I guess you have to choose the lesser of the two evils."

She looked as if she had actually shrunk in stature and had simultaneously become even thinner and more transparent. Sighing deeply, she began to pick at the upholstery with her fingers. Deep wrinkles began to show around her mouth and across the bridge of her nose. Suddenly Jenny understood what Mariann meant when she said that it wouldn't accomplish anything.

To her great surprise Mrs. Lidman went on to say, "You are probably right. I undoubtedly have to bear my own cross for Mariann's sake. I'll try not to be worried. But I know I'll worry anyway. I really have no control over that, you see. But go ahead and ride together. Tell Mariann that it's all right. I was only thinking about her welfare in the first place."

Arising unexpectedly, she took very small steps as she made her way straight across the room. She stood by a window, which was almost a green forest of indoor plants. Jenny knew that Mrs. Lidman had spoken the truth—that it was Mariann's welfare that had caused her actions. Jenny herself was certainly no longer in Mrs. Lidman's thoughts.

But what did all this mean? It meant that Jenny had won. Won!

"Thank you so much!" she said in conclusion as she moved toward the door. "I realize what a sacrifice you are making. But Mariann will be . . . ecstatic."

"Thank *you*, Jenny. I'm awfully glad that you and Mariann can be together," said Mrs. Lidman. But she didn't turn around.

Almost staggering, Jenny shut the door behind her. Now that it was over and done, she felt no triumph—only a slight emptiness. The emptiness, however, soon gave way to a great wave of relief. The mission had been accomplished. Now to tell Mariann.

CHAPTER 16

Jenny, Mariann, and Kristofer

"It worked!" was all that Jenny said when she opened the door to Mariann's room. "It worked. Don't you understand?"

Mariann, who was standing by her desk, turned around completely.

"Worked?" she said without an ounce of comprehension.

"Yes, worked. You're going to be allowed to ride. Your mother said . . . oh, well, it doesn't matter what she said. But you have her permission. You can ride again."

At last Mariann understood. Within a couple of seconds her entire countenance had been transformed. The dimples returned. It became the same vibrant, lively face that Jenny had remembered. Altogether unexpectedly, they found themselves face to face, their hands on each other's shoulders, their feet hopping and leaping in a dance of sheer joy.

"How did you behave?" Mariann began breathlessly, stopping as abruptly as she had begun. "What did you *say?*"

"Nothing special. Nothing, really. Only that you were bored. . . . But Mariann, why are we standing here talking. Come on, let's go to the stables."

Mariann stuck her head into her closet. The hanger

and the lovely new dress crashed to the floor, but she paid no attention to it. Instead she dug in a little deeper and emerged, laughing merrily, swinging a big sack around wildly.

"What's that?"

"Apples. Small, hard apples. Too green to eat, you understand. But Rascal loves them. I always have one with me in my pocket," said Mariann as she slipped into her red parka.

"Aha!" said Jenny.

In the hallway and down the stairs they kept up a steady stream of chatter. Mariann flew in to see her mother. Jenny stood and smiled as she looked at the closed door. She heard the jubilant shouts from Mariann, which almost drowned out her mother's subdued, controlled voice.

Presently they were out on the road. They didn't hurry as much as usual. They stopped now and then, sometimes just to talk, sometimes to kick pieces of ice at imaginary targets. But then they would suddenly break into a run, and it didn't take them long to reach their destination.

Suddenly Mariann halted.

"Jenny," she said. "I've been meaning to ask you about one important thing—where in the world did you get that revolver? Was it a real one?"

"Revolver?" Jenny asked in surprise. "What revolver?"

"The one you had in the stall, naturally," Mariann replied. "You and Lars. I almost had a heart attack. Were you really going to shoot?"

"Shoot?" Jenny said, just as perplexed as before. "What do you. . . . Oh! I know. Mariann, it was just Lars talking in his sleep—about Tumba Johansson and some crazy ice-hockey match."

They arrived at the stables almost helpless with laughter. There in the doorway stood Kristofer. He was wearing his riding habit and his heavy Icelandic sweater.

"Look who's here!" he cried. "Our long-lost prodigal daughter Mariann."

"I'm going in the office and ask about the free times and try to make an appointment," said Mariann, a little embarrassed by Kristofer's inquisitive glances. She disappeared into the office.

But Jenny stayed. Her eyes danced and her warm chestnut-brown hair glistened to such an extent that the harshness of the descending winter twilight seemed to give way to joy and brightness. She tried to sound sure of herself and serious when she said, "Have you looked at Rascal? She has a sprain, you know."

"She is no more sprained than you and Mariann are," Kristofer said dryly. "Say, that certainly is a bright red parka she has, isn't it?"

"Yes," Jenny answered. "Yes, it is." She stared downward, focusing particular attention on Kristofer's long boots and his gigantic feet—quite in proportion to the rest of his body. "Can you imagine," she continued. "We have everything arranged perfectly, Mariann and I. I am going to try to bring up my grades in composition and math, and she is going to help me with Rascal when I don't have enough time to take her out."

"Mariann rides awfully well," said Kristofer discreetly. "What mornings of the week is she going to have Rascal?"

Jenny looked up wide-eyed.

"I don't know," she said in surprise. "We haven't decided yet."

"Well, at least I got you to look at me," said Kristofer with no warning whatsoever. "I asked so that I could determine what days I wanted to be here myself. It's you I want to see on Rascal. You have some features in common. Your wide-set eyes, the color of your hair."

Jenny could sense that he was looking at her hair. She became so confused that she lost the thread of the conversation.

"I'm going to go in and say hello to Rascal," she said quickly.

Kristofer stayed back, watching her go through the stable door. With a tiny twinge of disappointment he noticed that her legs now filled out the legs of her riding breeches. There were no more wrinkles. She no longer reminded him of a deserted baby elephant.

"I wonder," he thought. "I wonder if she comes up to my shoulder."

Hastily he decided to go after her. He felt compelled to measure.